W9-CFO-003

rcp

CONSEQUENCE

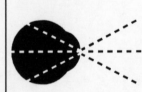

CONSEQUENCE

HAZEL STATHAM

THORNDIKE PRESS
A part of Gale, Cengage Learning

GALE
CENGAGE Learning·

Detroit • New York • San Francisco • New Haven, Conn • Waterville, Maine • London

LIBRARY OF CONGRESS CATALOGING-IN-PUBLICATION DATA

Statham, Hazel.
   Consequences / by Hazel Statham.
     p. cm. — (Thorndike Press large print gentle romance)
   ISBN-13: 978-1-4104-4285-7 (hardcover)
   ISBN-10: 1-4104-4285-3 (hardcover)
   1. Aristocracy (Social class)—England—Fiction. 2. England—Social life and customs—18th century—Fiction. 3. Large type books. I. Title.
PS3619.T3823C66 2012
813'.6—dc23   2011039179

Published in 2012 by arrangement with Thomas Bouregy & Co., Inc.

CONSEQUENCE

CONSEQUENCE

CHAPTER ONE

London 1748

It was a cold, gray December morning as three solitary figures stood quietly waiting in a coppice some five miles south of London. One, a young gentleman of twenty-two, paced silently back and forth, anxiously watching the road. As the first flakes of snow began to fall, he gazed up at the heavily laden sky and hoped the light would last.

One of his companions hailed him. "Good day for a duel, Lawrence," he said, with a heartiness he was far from feeling. "I've bespoken breakfast at The Pheasant, so I hope Lear don't keep us waiting too long." As he received no response, he continued to press his companion. "You won't forget the soirée at Lady Stanway's tonight, will you?"

"I won't," replied the young man, a flicker of a smile on his ghostly countenance. He suddenly started as a curricle and pair swept into view and, with sinking heart, he watched its approach.

The horses' breath froze into small clouds about their nostrils as they halted some yards away from the waiting trio, only the sound of their impatient hooves pervading the somber silence. His Grace, the Duke of Lear, a tall, dark, powerful man of twenty-nine, with mocking green eyes set beneath slightly winged brows, alighted from the driving seat and handed the reins to his groom, telling him to walk the horses out of sight.

The duke viewed the company with a bored indifference and giving a sardonic smile, drawled, "I find a late arrival the most effective, don't you?" Seeing Sir Lawrence look questioningly toward the road, he said, "Have no fear, my seconds follow in my wake. Lord Strafford's horse cast a shoe farther down the lane detaining him. However, the delay will be but slight, I do assure you." He strolled forward, slowly drawing off his driving gloves. "Have you the pistols, Lawrence?" he asked.

"But of course," replied Sir Lawrence, slightly inclining his head toward a rose-wood case in the hands of his second.

This gentleman suddenly started forward. "Your grace . . . ," he stammered.

The duke raised an enquiring brow, a

8

menacing gleam in his eye.

"As you know, sir," continued the second haltingly, "it is my first duty to try to bring about a reconciliation —"

"My dear sir, pray do not put yourself into such a taking," interrupted the duke. "It is not my usual practice to settle affairs of honor with young gentlemen of, shall we say, so few years, but as it is I who am the challenged, it is hardly my place to offer an apology."

"Devil take you, Lear," expostulated Sir Lawrence, starting forward with fists clenched at his side. "I have your measure, and my years need not concern you. As to apologizing, how does one offer his apologies to a notorious rake and gamester, a damned rakehell, who has the audacity to trifle with his sister?"

"A mere folly," assured his grace, languidly surveying a large sapphire on his left hand. "I assure you that if I hadn't been a trifle foxed at the time, I would not have entertained the idea. If I remember correctly, she is not what I would call a diamond of the first water. A mere chit, barely out of the schoolroom."

At this scarcely veiled insult, Sir Lawrence once again started forward, but his second placed a restraining hand on his arm and whispered words of caution.

Paying no heed, Lawrence stood defiantly before the duke, his countenance distorted with anger. "I see no reason why we must await the arrival of your seconds, Lear," he seethed through clenched teeth. "Let us have this matter over as soon as possible."

"Hold hard, my young fire-eater," said the duke in an infuriatingly calm tone. "Unless my eyes deceive me, I perceive the very gentlemen you wish to exclude from this happy gathering." Turning, he called to one of the approaching horse men: "Come, do not dawdle, Strafford. This young bantam is eager to see the color of my blood, which, I hasten to assure, is quite as black as he believes it to be."

The Duke of Lear's two seconds dismounted and joined the gathering. "I have arranged for a doctor to arrive at precisely half after eight," informed Lord Strafford. "Therefore, gentlemen, I propose that we waste no more time, as we have but ten minutes to enact the affair. If you will allow me to inspect the pistols, we can commence."

The weapons duly inspected, each of the duelists made his choice and then, standing back to back, listened to the conditions of the engagement.

Lord Strafford stepped forward. "On my count, gentlemen, you will each take ten paces forward and turn and fire on command. Either man firing before the given signal, if he misses his target, must stand and let the other discharge his weapon without defense. However, if he should wound or kill his opponent, it is my duty to shoot him. Now, gentlemen, if you are ready, *one, two, three* . . ." His words rang out clearly, sounding ominously loud in the ears of the duelists. *"Eight, nine, ten."* Both men turned. *"FIRE!"*

Two shots rang out simultaneously, one burying itself in the trunk of a nearby tree, the other finding its mark in the chest of Sir Lawrence, who pitched forward onto the hardened ground, and all was silent and still.

After what seemed an age, the duke's pistol arm dropped to his side and he stood gazing at the inert body with an expression of compassion. "I think I have missed the heart," he said, forgetting to drawl. "I aimed somewhat to the right. If you would but remove him to his carriage, we can endeavor to make him comfortable until the surgeon arrives."

No one spoke, but Sir Lawrence's seconds moved forward and, raising his body, carried it to the waiting coach.

It was true, he was not dead, but the tie of life seemed very weak. A flask of brandy was put to his purple lips, but the liquid merely ran out the corners of his mouth.

Lord Strafford drew the duke aside. "I think you had better be on your way, Marcel," he said. "It's a damnable affair, and it would not be prudent for the doctor to see you."

"Devil a bit," replied his grace. "The foolish young pup should have known better than to call me out. My reputation goes before me. Let me know how he fares, will you? I will be at my club tonight."

"I will call in as soon as I have any news," assured his lordship. "Now for sanity's sake, be gone, Marcel."

With a curt nod of his head, the duke strode away to the other side of the coppice, where his groom was walking the horses. Leaping into the driving seat, he took the reins, springing his horses forward, barely giving his man time to jump up behind him, only slackening his pace as he reached the outskirts of London.

That evening, when Lord Strafford went in search of the duke, he found him at a table given up to Deep Basset at his club in St. James'.

His grace was dressed in a full-skirted coat of dove-gray velvet, heavily laced with silver, with satin knee breeches of the same hue. The finest Dresden lace foamed at his throat and fell over his long, slender hands. His raven locks were powdered, and a diamond buckle was placed over the black ribbon that confined them. His face was innocent of the powder and patches affected by the Macaronis, and he even disdained the hare's foot and rouge. Diamond clips adorned his lacquered shoes and, to complete the effect, a jeweled dress sword hung at his side.

At that moment, his grace was holding the bank against a very worried-looking gentleman in a bagwig, but as soon as the duke spied Strafford, he brought the game to a swift and profitable conclusion.

"What news?" he asked, joining his lordship in one of the curtained antechambers.

"I haven't seen the lad, Marcel, but news has it he may not last the night. It was a damnable business, y'know. Wouldn't be surprised if you don't hear from the magistrate before morning. That is, if you're still here."

The duke, arms folded, had been steadfastly gazing at the floor, but at these last few words he raised his head and fixing his companion with a steel-like gaze repeated, "If I'm still here? May I ask why I should not be here? It was clearly my life or his, and I find I think mine the more valuable."

"That ain't the point, though," said his lordship, coloring slightly beneath the duke's scrutiny. "Lawrence was so young . . ."

"Young enough to issue a challenge. It was not I who instigated the duel."

Strafford shrugged. "Fact is, y'can't do with any more scandal. You have the name of Blake to uphold. Would make it very uncomfortable for your family if Lawrence dies. If you would only leave the country for a while, the matter can be settled out of hand."

"I see," said the duke sardonically, now thoroughly enlightened. "It is not my skin that you are worried about, but the fair name of Blake, and as you are soon to be married into the family, you have no mind to have a relative branded as a murderer." Then, with a hardening of his countenance: "Very well, I will go to France so that my esteemed sister can marry you with a clear conscience. Allow me to offer you my felicitations, and now *bonne nuit.* I will be on my way to Dieppe by the morning tide."

Turning on his heel, Marcel swept out of

the alcove and into the smoky atmosphere of the gaming rooms. He was hailed by one or two of his cronies, who invited him to join their set, but he curtly refused their offers and made his way into the forehall where he collected his cane, cloak, and tricorn. The footman who held the street door for him asked if he must call his carriage, but his grace declined, preferring, in this mood, to walk the short distance to his townhouse.

A thin layer of snow covered the ground as the duke made his way out of St James'. He had a deal of arranging to do before morning. Luckily, his yacht, *The Copper Mistress,* was always held in readiness so, if he did not miss the morning tide, he could be in Dieppe the following evening. There would be no problem where transport was concerned, for his grace held teams of horses at strategic points on the main route to the coast.

As he strode through dimly lit streets, his thoughts reverted back to the cause of the duel, and he bit off a laugh of self-scorn. He had been in his cups when he encountered Lawrence's younger sister, Leticia. The forward young miss had escaped unnoticed from her parents' home to join her military escort and partake in the delights of a masked ball at a notorious hall known for passionate encounters. While her beau had sought out refreshments, the young lady in question had set about exploring the hall, and it was then that she had drawn the duke's attention. He had been halfheartedly paying court to a vivacious beauty but, upon the return of her gallant, was not averse to setting up a flirtation with a more available partner. Leticia promised such a diversion as, forgetting her escort and believing her identity safe behind her mask, she had openly courted the duke's interest. Being experienced in the art of dalliance, it had not taken the duke long to persuade her to join him in a less frequented part of the building. It was as they traversed one of the quieter corridors that they were halted by Sir Lawrence, who had been apprised of his sister's actions by one of his acquaintances, who had spied her alighting from her escort's carriage. The young lord had wasted no time in setting out in her wake, his temper rising with each passing moment of his search. Meeting her in the duke's company had finally brought it to a head, and he had immediately issued his challenge, which had been accepted with a mocking bow.

Presented with the choice of weapons the

following morning, Marcel instructed his seconds to state pistols as his choice. He thought them more accurate, allowing him to take the element of chance from the encounter. It had not been his intention to wound the young lord, merely to prove how rash had been his actions. Had not Lawrence shifted his position in the final second that their shots were discharged, honor would have been satisfied without bloodshed.

Now, when he looked back on the episode, he realized how foolhardy the whole affair had been. He should not have allowed himself to be drawn into a duel, the outcome of which was only too predictable, and he cursed himself soft and long for being a fool. A fool whose actions had cost him dearly and now necessitated his removal to France.

When he reached Blake House, an impassive butler opened the door immediately.

"Send my valet to me," ordered the duke, relinquishing his cloak and hat into this worthy's care. "Tell the groom to have the light traveling chaise at the door in an hour. I intend leaving London for a while," and at this, he repaired to his bedchamber.

Marcel was just brushing his hair free of

powder when Oakes, his valet, scratched on the door. "You wanted to see me, your grace," he said, coming into the center of the room. He was somewhat surprised at being summoned at this late hour, for it was usually the duke's wont to dispense with his services after visiting his club, or his current light-o-love.

Marcel glanced but briefly at the small, wiry valet who had been in his employ for more than a decade. "We go to France immediately, Oakes. Lay out my traveling habit and pack whatever is needed for a lengthy stay. Do not dawdle; we leave within the hour."

"Very well, sir," replied Oakes. He had known the duke too long to be in any way perturbed by any order he should receive, and he made haste to do his grace's bidding. His own preparations would take but a few minutes to complete, so he was able to devote his time to the packing and, with the help of one of the lackeys, managed to be ready in time.

The hall clock struck one as his grace went through the front door. He stood for a moment at the top of the steps, giving a few last instructions to his majordomo before entering the coach, Oakes following hastily

18

in his wake. As the vehicle moved away from Blake House, Oakes ventured a question: "May I inquire where in France we go, sir?"

"Paris," was the short, sharp reply that discouraged any further discourse as Marcel gazed pensively out the window, watching the dim outlines of the houses as they made their way through the streets. Once clear of London, he gave the order to make all haste and the coachman sprang the horses on the deserted roads, heading for Newhaven.

Inside the coach, wrapped in a fur-lined cloak, his grace began to doze in the shadows of the corner. Slowly his tricorn slipped over his forehead and, stretching his long legs out in front of him, he thrust his hands deep into his breeches pockets, the swaying of the well-sprung coach affecting him not at all.

Just as the gray light of dawn crept through formidable clouds, the coach was brought to a slithering halt outside one of the quay-side taverns. Oakes secretly quaked as he saw how the sharp wind whipped along the wharf and tossed the craft in the harbor, but he said not a word to his employer. He would not risk the duke's ire.

Marcel roused himself and after stretching sent his valet to procure a private parlor at the tavern, where he could partake of breakfast. This being accomplished, his grace stepped languidly down from the coach, and with an air of condescension made his way into the hired room where his valet awaited him.

The duke appeared in a more amiable mood as he said, "When breakfast is served, Oakes, ask the captain of *The Copper Mistress* to join me here. Tell him I wish to set sail with the tide."

With countenance of stone, Oakes left the comforts of the inn to brave the driving sleet of the quay.

Left alone, the duke seated himself at the head of the table. Showing no more than a fleeting interest in the meal of beef and ale set before him, he sat back in his chair, savoring the warmth of the large log fire that had been set for his benefit. He still felt drowsy, and the warmth was a welcome contrast to the chills of his conveyance. He had had no time to send a servant ahead to prepare the Hôtel Lear in Paris, but his grace was confident that he could put up at his cousin's hotel until the lackeys could remove the covers. He was still musing on the reception he would receive when he should arrive at cousin Stefan's when a knock sounded on the parlor door.

"Enter," commanded his grace, straightening himself in his seat.

A tall, bearded individual entered and removed his cap as he crossed the threshold, his weather-beaten countenance proclaiming him the captain of *The Copper Mistress.*

"Ah, Mayer," said his grace. "I trust all is well, and we will be able to catch the tide?"

"Begging your grace's pardon," said Mayer, "but I wouldn't advise attempting a crossing in this weather. The wind's fair tearing at the *Mistress* as it is. Perhaps if we waited for the evening tide, she might be able to hold her own, but as it is now, I couldn't swear we would reach Dieppe in one piece."

"That, my friend, is a risk we have to take," drawled the duke.

"If your grace says so, but . . ."

"I do say so," said the duke, in such a tone that Mayer was left in no doubt of his meaning, precluding any further debate on the subject.

"Aye, aye, sir. We heave to in twenty minutes." So saying, the captain departed, leaving the duke to his meal.

When the duke stepped out onto the quayside, the wind whipped his cloak about his legs and stung his face with its salty spray.

The Copper Mistress rose and fell with the swell of the waves, looking like some monstrous fish as her bows dipped precariously. The duke beckoned to Oakes, who was sheltering in the doorway to the tavern, and, raising his voice above the blast, asked, "Is everything aboard?"

"Yes, sir," replied the valet, joining his master. "Everything is stowed below."

"Then we depart," said his grace, leading the way up the gangplank.

The deck of the yacht swayed heavily under their feet as the duke and Oakes witnessed the setting of the sails and the weighing of anchor, but they had only just passed the harbor mouth when Oakes hesitantly touched the duke's sleeve.

"If it pleases, your grace," he said with some effort of composure, "I will go below until you have further need of me. I find this mode of travel slightly discomposing."

"By all means go below," said the duke, surveying the woebegone figure before him with some amusement. "I can see you're feeling somewhat green about the gills." Producing a small flask from his coat pocket, he gave it to his valet, saying, "Take this with you. It may help to settle your palate."

Clasping the flask to his chest, Oakes

bowed gratefully and wasted no time in disappearing down the companionway.

Watching his departure with some amusement, his grace went to stand in the bows of the ship as she entered the open channel, the movement of the vessel seeming not to affect him in any way. Mayer was at the wheel and plied the *Mistress* through the beating waves, whose whitecaps swelled onto the deck, drenching the duke's boots, but his grace, riveting his gaze on the stormy horizon, was oblivious of the elements.

Soon the sleet changed to snow that almost immediately became an impregnable blind, and the vessel had to be guided by instinct rather than sight. One of the crew pleaded with the duke to go below before he was swept overboard, but it took all his powers of persuasion to get him to consent. It was with a great show of reluctance that the duke left his post and made his way across the heaving deck.

He swung down the companionway into the small corridor onto which the three main cabins opened, one of which was occupied by the now very seasick Oakes. Marcel looked in on this unfortunate individual but, as Oakes showed no visible signs of gaining his sea legs, left him in the very capable hands of a cabin boy.

Entering the main apartment, his grace removed his now soaking cloak and flung it negligently over a chair. There was nothing for him to do but to take his ease for the remainder of the journey, and, remembering that his cupboard always revealed a bottle of good brandy, he wasted no time in availing himself of its warming benefits. Seating himself in a heavy leather chair, which was well secured to the heaving timbers, he resigned himself to the tedium of the crossing.

The cabin was slightly larger than its two companions. There were four portholes, but on such a stormy day as this, the main source of light was supplied by an oil lamp suspended in the center of the ceiling. The lamp swung back and forth with each movement, casting grotesque shadows to either side. A table was set to the right of the cabin, its legs firmly screwed to the planking to keep it in place, and a curtained bunk was set against the ribs. It was here that his grace finally decided to seek repose, the brandy and movement of the ship lulling him into a heavy slumber.

CHAPTER TWO

The wavelets lapped gently against the *Mistress* as she lay anchored in the dimly lit harbor of Dieppe. The wind had dropped, and the snow had changed to a steady fall of icy rain. Oakes, now fully recovered, made his way to his master's cabin, tapping lightly on the door and, upon receiving a somewhat drowsy reply, cautiously entered. As he gazed at the duke lying abed, he uttered a startled cry.

"What's to do now?" expostulated his grace, starting to a sitting position in his bunk.

"Sir," said the valet in despairing tones, almost forcing the words from between clenched teeth. "You have lain down in your coat, and it is now quite ruined. I have known gentlemen who would rather die of cold than use their raiment so. You must forgive me, sir, for speaking plainly, but you have sorely misused that which it is my duty to —"

"Enough, enough," said his grace with a laugh, amused by the look of horror on his valet's dour countenance. "You must not take such a pet, Oakes. I'm sure my coat has sustained no lasting injury, and I have every faith in your excellent ability to put it to rights."

Oakes heaved a heavy sigh. His offended gaze came to rest on the cloak cast negligently over the chair, but upon encountering a forbidding look from his employer, he said no more but lovingly removed the crumpled garment and ineffectually attempted to smooth out the creases. Casting a wounded glance at his master, he inquired, "When will your grace be wishing to go ashore?"

The duke rose from the bunk and shook out his ruffles, carefully rearranging his neck-cloth. "I will be ready to go ashore as soon as you present me with a change of coat," he said, taking out his snuffbox and tapping it lightly. "I trust you will not keep me waiting too long, Oakes."

The valet bowed himself out, to return a few moments later carrying a fresh coat, which, still wearing a look of injury on his tired features, he presented for the duke's approval.

The duke's eyes narrowed. "Oakes," he reproved in menacing tones. "I warn you, I will brook no insolence. I grow tired of the matter. Let it drop, and cast that look off your already sour visage."

Realizing that he had driven his master too far, and uttering profound apologies, Oakes helped the duke shrug into his coat.

"I have decided to reside at *Le Chien Noir* for the evening," said his grace, drawing on his gloves. "You will precede me there and bespeak the required apartments, and also inquire where a coach and horses may be hired for our journey on the morrow. I will join you at the inn when I have spoken to Mayer, so be sure that everything is as it should be."

Wishing to remain in his master's good graces, Oakes hurried up on deck and along the quayside whose cobbles, made slippery by the falling rain, glinted dimly in the fitful light of a watery moon. The inn was a large-fronted building frequented by personages of rank and fortune where one could always be sure of comfortable, clean accommodation blended with good food and wine.

The landlord, recognizing a nobleman's valet when he saw one, greeted Oakes amicably and, speaking in good English,

27

said, "In what way may I have the honor of serving you, *m'sieur?*"

Oakes had a very poor opinion of the French, for what man in his right mind would attempt a meal of snails? Drawing himself to his full height, he replied with great dignity, "I require apartments for my master, His Grace, the Duke of Lear, and also a room for myself. His grace will require supper immediately when he arrives, and it should be served in his private parlor."

The welcoming smile disappeared from the landlord's mien, and a haughty look took its place. He had no liking for this insolent English servant. He recognized the name of the servant's master, however, and was reluctant to turn away such a notable personage. "It shall be as you wish," he said coldly, snapping his fingers to dispatch various lackeys to their tasks. "All will be in readiness to receive his grace, the *most noble duc.*" His sneer was pronounced when he added, "I have but one small room remaining that is suitable for you."

Oakes followed in the landlord's wake to rooms on the first floor. After asserting that the apartment, consisting of a private parlor, bedroom, and dressing room, would be to the duke's liking, and feeling sorely in need of refreshment, he betook himself to the taproom before his master should arrive.

Thus it was that the duke entered the inn quite unattended a short while later. He presented a very formidable figure as he stood on the threshold, surveying the interior through his quizzing glass. His eye alighted on two cloaked figures standing at the foot of the stairs, their portmanteaux at their feet, but then the landlord hurrying forward claimed his attention.

"I see," said his grace, once more raising his glass to survey a blank wall, "that you have removed the painting that so offended my sight the last time I was here. I compliment you on your good taste."

"But of course, *Monseigneur*," replied the landlord, bowing, "for it was your expert knowledge that guided my hand." Spreading wide his arm, he indicated the staircase. "If your grace would be so kind as to follow me, I will take you to your apartments."

"By-the-bye, where is my valet?" inquired the duke in displeased tones. "He was to await me here."

"That, *Monseigneur*, I cannot answer," replied the landlord, "but I will inquire after him and send him to your grace posthaste." At this he turned to lead the duke to his rooms, but just as his grace was about to mount the stairs, one of the cloaked figures stretched out a timid hand and touched his sleeve.

Marcel swung around to see who dared accost him, but his surprised gaze alighted on the slight figure of a young girl enveloped in a large traveling cloak. His quick retort died on his lips, and instead he raised an enquiring brow.

"Pray excuse me, sir," said the girl in unsure tones, her eyes, shadowed by the hood of the cloak, making her face but a pale oval. "I hope you will forgive me for making so bold as to speak, but with you lies the decision as to whether my maid and I shall stay under a roof this night or be turned away."

Without hesitation, the duke made a profound leg. "Dear ma'am, I will assist you in any way possible," he said, reverently bowing over the tiny hand extended to him. There was a hint of mockery in his voice, but the girl seemed not to notice. "If you will but tell me how I may serve you, I will endeavor to do so."

"Thank you, sir," she replied, a slight smile hovering on her lips. "You and your man have taken the only rooms left at the inn, and as there is no other accommodation, my maid and I will be forced to travel to the next town. As it is already quite late, we fear it to be impossible. I was wondering, therefore, sir, if perhaps you would have a truckle bed set up in your dressing room for your valet so that we may have his room."

Without replying, the duke turned to the landlord, saying, "You will, of course, make the necessary arrangements." Losing all interest in the situation, he bowed and prepared to take his leave, but once again the delicate hand detained him. "Yes?" he inquired with forced civility as he once more turned to face the girl. He longed for the comforts of his hired room and was impatient of the delay.

Her countenance colored under his sardonic gaze, but she met his look steadily. "I would like to thank you, sir, and also to inquire of your name, for I can hardly accept such kindness from a complete stranger!"

"Marcel, Duke of Lear, at your service," he replied lightly, a spark of interest igniting despite his irritation. There was something in the girl's cultured tones that caught his attention, and he once again made a slight bow. "Ah, but now, madam, you have the advantage over me. I can hardly *extend* such kindness to a complete stranger."

A gurgle of laughter escaped her. "You mock me, sir," she cried, not entirely unaware that his interest was piqued. "However, I shall pay you no heed. I am Julie Markham." Then, turning on her heel and catching her skirts, she hurried away up the stairs in the wake of a waiting lackey, thus preventing any further discourse.

With a slight shrug, the duke followed the landlord to his apartment.

The landlord had just taken leave of the duke after ensuring that everything was as it should be when Oakes nervously entered the parlor. His grace stood nonchalantly surveying the valet, but the duke's calm exterior belied a fast-rising anger betrayed only by a white line around his already grim lips. "I trust I do not disturb you from your drinking," he said in deceptively silky tones. "I would not wish you to be put out on my account. Pray be seated, and I will serve your ale to you in my parlor."

"Your grace must forgive me," said Oakes, visibly writhing under the duke's fiery gaze. "It was not my intention to remain overlong in the taproom, but I was talking to someone who knew where we could hire a suitable conveyance for tomorrow's journey."

"You are so solicitous of our comforts," scorned the duke, "but would it not be best to attend to this evening's needs before the morrow's? You not only desert your post so that I am obliged to see to my own arrival, but you go so far as to wait a full half hour before presenting yourself. In the meantime, I have reordered supper, searched through my portmanteaux for suitable evening clothes, and given your room to two young ladies. Therefore, you will need to set up a truckle bed in my dressing room. Your conduct today has left a great deal to be desired. I trust I need not refer to the matter again. However, should it become necessary, I will feel compelled to relieve myself of your services. I hope I make myself clear."

"Perfectly, your grace," replied a very pale Oakes. "I will endeavor to render myself once more worthy of your trust."

At that moment, the lackeys entered to lay the covers for supper, and further discourse between master and valet was impossible. When the meal was over and the duke was settled beside the fire, however, no more was said about Oakes' misconduct. In fact, the duke was in quite an amiable mood, notwithstanding he was a trifle foxed, but in this condition he was always at his most pleasant. He sat for some while over his brandy, slowly turning the glass in his hand and watching the flames of a large log fire reflect in its rich depths before finally, as the clock struck half after twelve, retiring to bed.

Oakes settled himself in the dressing room, content with the thought that he had at least secured the only conveyance worthy of transporting an English *duc* and his cortège to the French capital.

By morning, the rain had ceased and the wind had dropped to a light breeze. Oakes was the first to rise, and he drew back the curtains of his small closet with a sigh of relief. At least today he would not be called upon to brave the extremities of the Channel. Although away from London and on the road, his master still expected his boots to have a mirrorlike shine, and so Oakes set about this task before the duke should awaken and demand his services.

It was almost ten o'clock before the duke bestirred himself, and then it was with some reluctance, for the brandy he had drunk the previous night had had a druglike effect on him, but never was his grace known to suffer a hangover. It was therefore with a clear brain that he received the attentions of his valet in assisting him to dress.

When the time came for his grace to set out on the road to Paris, the landlord ventured to ask his opinion of a new seascape being hung in the hallway, and after receiving some mild applause was quite content, assuring his grace of his undying gratitude for both his opinion and his patronage.

Entering the coach, the duke was not aware that he was the object of scrutiny, as Miss Markham witnessed his departure from the window of her bedroom, which overlooked the cobbled roadway. Dalliance being the furthest thought from his mind, he would have cared naught had he seen her. Knowing the route his journey must take, the only desire he would admit to was to reach his cousin's home and therefore the comforts of his hearth; not for the first time, the duke cursed his actions that had made his journey necessary. Despite his reputation, he was not such a hardened rakehell as was generally perceived, and although he would never admit to it, he bore a conscience.

It was two o'clock on the third day that the equipage finally rumbled through the streets of Paris. For all that the weather was chill, the streets thronged with people, the walls throbbing with their laughter and tears, to all of which the duke was an uninterested spectator.

The coach, after passing through what its occupant thought mile upon mile of sordid back streets, finally came to the more fashionable part of the city. Here the streets were wider but no less crowded. Carriages and sedan chairs filled the roadway while, despite the bitter weather, the *monde* moved leisurely along the pavements. The coach took a sudden turning left into a less crowded street; this was *la rue Fleuret,* where Mr. Stefan Blake, the duke's cousin, resided. The horses halted before an impressive-looking building some three stories high, with large sash windows overlooking a small but neat square.

His grace, not waiting for the groom to let down the steps, leaped nimbly down and, crossing to the large front door, raised the heavy knocker. Almost immediately, a lackey of quite some years opened the door and, perceiving the duke, something resembling a smile lit his grizzled countenance. "Your grace," he said, bowing. "It is so good to see you again. Mr. Blake is in the library reading over the papers. If you would but allow me a moment, I will announce you."

Smiling, his grace stepped into the hall.

"No need for that, Maunders. I will announce myself." So saying, he handed his tricorn and cane to the faithful lackey, but declined the suggestion that he remove his cloak. "I may have to leave in a hurry," he confided wryly, a light of amusement in his eye. The duke and his cousin had had a slight misunderstanding over a delightful mademoiselle on his last visit to Paris, and he was far less than certain of his reception.

Quietly, the duke opened the library door and stole unnoticed to the back of his cousin's chair. Being engrossed in the daily journal and having his back to the door, Stefan Blake had not noticed his visitor's entrance and continued reading for some moments before his grace made his presence known by reading aloud a passage over his shoulder. "A most interesting piece of scandal, coz, don't you think?" he said, lightly putting his hand on his cousin's shoulder.

Startled, Stefan sprang up from his chair. "You!" he expostulated. "What the deuce are *you* doing here?"

"Ah, I knew I should not have come," said the duke in mock dismay. "I will go directly, for now even you have cast me off."

Stefan laughed, briefly gripping his cousin's arms. "Marcel, you fool. You know I'm always deuced glad to see you. Here, take that damned cloak off and join me in a glass of claret." So saying, he turned his attention to pouring the wine.

Stefan was some two years the duke's senior but with far less sense. He was generally known as a veritable coxcomb, or cat's whisker, among the gentlemen, and a great flirt with the ladies. He was of slender build, but some six inches or so shorter than the duke; his flaxen hair, which always remained powdered, was a severe contrast to his estimable cousin's raven locks. He also, much to his grace's disgust, adorned his mien with not only one but two patches, one high on his right cheek and the other at the left corner of his mouth. His turnout with swords was considered pretty but ineffectual, but, as many would reluctantly admit, he was a bruising good rider.

His grace, divest of his cloak, joined Stefan around the fire and, sinking into a large armchair, stretched his booted feet to the hearth and received his claret gratefully.

"What brings you here at this inhospitable time of year, Marcel?" asked Stefan, resuming his seat. "Don't get the idea that I'm not glad to see you. Fact is, I'm devilishly glad. I'm in dire need of company other than my own; but when you come to Paris out of season, there is always some underlying reason. Remember a year or two ago, the same thing happened, devilishly tricky situation —"

"Enough said," pleaded the duke. "Don't start dragging that up again. Fact is, had a duel and killed my man."

"Killed him?"

"He was as good as dead when I left England."

"Stupid thing to do, Marcel. What if he had killed you? If this duel was fought honorably — and if I know you, you would countenance nothing less — why flee London?"

"There you have the nub of it. He was naught but a youth. I should have had more sense and ignored his challenge, but the young hothead would insist on the match. Strafford persuaded me it was my duty to protect the family name. It appears that even I am not immune to censure."

"Surely your reputation in these matters goes before you. The lad was beyond foolish to press the issue. 'Twould appear you had no option. Swords or pistols?"

"Pistols."

"Indelicate, my dear coz. The sword is by far the superior. Always use it myself, though I can't boast as many hits as you."

"Didn't know you could boast of any," said the duke, raising a quizzical brow.

"Can't really," admitted Stefan reluctantly, "but one must appear to have some proficiency in the art. It's the done thing. Admit it: I nearly put one in over your guard last time we sparred, but my wrist ain't as strong as yours." Then, after a slight pause: "By-the-bye, I go to Gaultier's tonight. Its reputation as a fashionable gaming hell has been enhanced by royal patronage. Do you accompany me, or are you going to Hôtel Blake?"

His grace smiled ruefully. "This, I fear, is where my visit will become unwelcome. I was hoping you could put me up here until my townhouse is ready to receive me. Of course, if it is inconvenient, I could remove to one of the hotels, which I am led to believe are excellent, if somewhat over-crowded."

"No such thing," said Stefan, rising and pulling on the bell rope. "I'll be glad of your company. Maunders shall arrange for a room to be prepared for you. Pleased to see you, y'know, or have I already said that?"

"Yes!"

"Oh well, I'll say it again . . ."

The duke stifled a yawn, saying, "I pray you will not. It becomes wearisome."

"Fool," said Stefan, laughing. Then, as Maunders entered: "You will prepare my cousin's usual room. He is to stay indefinitely."

Maunders, not betraying by as much as a smile that he had anticipated the order some ten minutes earlier, bowed impassively and retired from the room feeling very well pleased with himself.

Stefan turned once more to his cousin, saying, "Do you come with me tonight, or has the journey fatigued you?"

The duke grinned. "Not a bit of it. I seem to have done nothing but sleep since we left London. What time do we start for Gaultier's?"

"First," sighed Stefan, "I am bound over to the British ambassador for supper. However, I should arrive, with luck — for the old gentleman is a veritable windbag — at about half after ten, so I will meet you there. Oh, yes, and tomorrow you shall come to Versailles with me. Have to go to court, you know. Devilishly boring, but there it is, and I'll be blowed if I'll suffer it alone. You shall put on your court manners and bear me company."

"Is The Pompadour still reigning supreme," queried his grace, "or has Louis found another bird to feather his nest?"

"She still rules supreme," grinned Stefan. "She has young D'aubigne in her toils. The young fool is always hanging on her skirts. Makes it too obvious. I know one thing: She'll be prodigiously glad to see you. Always happy to see a fresh face in court. Means one more conquest."

"Not I," said the duke, sobering. "I want to keep my head, and besides, she is not exactly to my liking."

"Just what is to your liking?" said Stefan, chuckling. "I never knew you had a particular brand of woman, as you would have a particular brand of snuff. Hardly the same. I myself prefer variety."

"What, in snuff?"

"No, women!"

The duke gave a bark of laughter. "Your taste in women never ceases to amaze me. If truth be told, there has only ever been one instance when I have been wholly in agreement with you —"

Raising his hand to halt any further reminiscences, Stefan grinned, saying, "If you are to remain under my roof, it is a time best forgotten."

Grinning in return, Marcel inclined his head. "Truce, cousin. All is forgotten."

If he looked to meet his cousin at Gaultier's

later that evening, the duke was destined for disappointment. Had he but known it, Stefan, in the company of the ambassador, was at that precise moment arriving at a remote farm on the outskirts of Paris. It had not taken much persuading on Lord Markham's part to convince his visitor to accompany him to the cock fight. Once the projected outing had been mentioned, all thoughts of his waiting cousin had fled Stefan's brain, and he had grabbed at the chance of witnessing the sport. Due to the press of people and vehicles in the lane, the progress of his lordship's coach was necessarily slow, but this in no way lessened their anticipation of the event.

Lord Markham, a small rotund man with a florid countenance, frequently peered out the window to check their progress. "The company might be a trifle low, but who cares, if the sport is good?" he enthused, well pleased with the projected sport and his companion.

Stefan appeared equally as eager. "It's an age since I last went cocking," he confessed. "Ratting's all the rage now, y'know, but it's not the same. Fact is, sport's been devilishly slow this season. It's the one thing I sorely miss when I'm this side of the Channel."

"You say Lear is staying with you?" said

his lordship. "Then both of you shall come to Sefron Towers for the Christmas festivities. My wife would never forgive me if I neglected to invite you. Just a few sporting friends, nothing grand. Got some new blood 'n' bones set up in m'stables, and you can hunt from there on the twenty-sixth. I'm sure we have something to take your fancy. Anything for a bit of sport, eh?"

Uncertain what his cousin's reaction would be to the invitation, Stefan nonetheless accepted. It had been almost a year since his last outing, and the promise of a day's hunting was just too tempting to resist.

Eventually the equipage rumbled over the cobbled yard of the farm. Several vehicles had already been drawn up outside a large wooden barn, with other gamesters still coming in from the road. His lordship and Stefan alighted and, with great anticipation, made their way into the barn's shadowy interior.

At first entering, Stefan put his heavily scented handkerchief to his nostrils, for, despite the chill of the night air, an odor of warm bodies and farmyard smells assailed his delicate senses. In the light of the lanterns, one could see the dust motes rising from the choppings of old hay that were spread over the floor, and scurryings in the remote corners proved that they were not the only inhabitants who sought warmth. In the center of the barn, a circle of about eight feet in diameter had been marked out, and a series of wooden forms and hay bales had been arranged in varying heights around it to serve as seating accommodation.

There didn't appear to be any seats left, but just as Stefan was beginning to despair of ever finding a vantage point, his lordship spied a space between a gentleman farmer and a man of uncertain occupation who was wearing a moleskin jacket. Reluctantly, Stefan took his place between Lord Markham and the farmer, subjecting his silk coat to the most unforgivable misuse, its skirts now nothing more than a crumpled mass.

Just as the crowd began to get impatient, the first pair of cockerels was brought to the edge of the ring. One was a red bird with a good breadth of chest and the other a gray whose heels were adorned by spurs. The owner of the red cock noticed these weapons and only after a heated argument with his opponent did he finally win his case and the spurs were removed.

"I'll wager you a monkey the red wins," said his lordship, giving Stefan a friendly dig in the ribs with his elbow. "I pride myself on being able to pick my bird," he boasted.

"I think the gray will have the advantage," countered Stefan. "He has less weight to carry." Suddenly he realized that the farmer was eyeing him rather askance. It appeared that Stefan had been noted by this worthy as one of *the quality*, his raiment not going entirely unnoticed.

"Is anything wrong, my dear fellow?" he asked, raising his quizzing glass to scrutinize the farmer's ruddy countenance.

"Non, m'lor," said the farmer, hastily averting his gaze.

A murmur running through the crowd heralded the setting of the cocks, and all eyes were riveted on the poorly lit circle. The handlers released the birds, and the two cockerels eyed each other warily. With feathers raised around the base of their necks, they sidled, each looking for an opening. Suddenly the red spied his chance and flew at its opponent. At this, audience members broke into an uproar, encouraging whichever bird took their fancy. Stefan held his tongue at first, but after perceiving his lordship giving full vent to his opinion, he, first hesitantly, and then heartily, added his voice to those shouting for the gray.

Feathers flew as the birds engaged once again. It was clear that the red was above holding his own, but the gray was by far the more nimble and managed to free itself from the red's claws. The atmosphere became intoxicating, lord and lad alike haggling over their champions. Lord Markham suddenly became embroiled in an argument with his neighbor while Stefan had a jug of home brew pressed upon him and drank deeply.

Somehow, the red managed to bestride the gray and was just going in for the kill when the handlers started forward, tearing the birds apart. It was, therefore, a triumph for the red, and also for Lord Markham, who heartily slapped Stefan on the back, once more proclaiming his knowledge of birds. Stefan, who was beginning to feel slightly fuddled, replied only in slurred accents, wiping his elegant sleeve across his brow.

The evening sped on, his lordship getting more and more elated as each of his predictions came true, and Stefan getting more and more foxed as he partook of the jug passing freely between himself and the farmer.

Eventually the match was over, and the excitement began to abate. His lordship viewed Stefan with a twinkle of amusement in his eye, for his young companion was looking very comical, with his elegantly powdered wig pushed to one side and his exquisite lace cravat limp and creased.

"Well, lad, you look a real peagoose," mocked the ambassador, taking hold of Stefan's arm. "Anyone would take you for a real Johnny Raw."

Stefan shrugged away his lordship's hand, for, unlike his cousin, he was not at his best when in his cups. "Go to the devil," he muttered darkly. "I've dropped enough blunt to buy Versailles, and all you can do is mock me. I can assure you, sir, I am no Johnny Raw."

"That's right, lad," agreed his lordship, deeming it best to humor him. "It's deuced late and time we returned to Paris."

Stefan refused any offer of assistance, made his way, though a trifle unsteadily, back to the coach, and gratefully sank back onto the mauve velvet squabs where, almost immediately, he fell asleep.

An hour later, Lord Markham's carriage finally drew up in *la rue Fleuret.* All was quiet, and the single street light shone eerily across the frost-spangled pavement. His lordship tried to wake Stefan, but his efforts were in effective, and after a few moments, he was obliged to alight from the carriage and raise the knocker to Stefan's hotel.

A very weary Maunders answered the summons. He had evidently been waiting for his master to return, but his countenance was devoid of the impatience that had mastered it not ten minutes earlier, for he had been trained not to show the slightest emotion on his impassive countenance. From the time Stefan had brought him, along with his other lackeys, from London, Maunders had counted himself head of the domestic staff. He had seen his master through two duels and several mistresses without wavering in his steadfast loyalty. Standing in the doorway, he listened indulgently to Lord Markham's explanation of Mr. Blake's condition and, summoning a sleepy porter stationed in the hallway, stepped out into the street to lift his master tenderly from the carriage. Conveying him up to his apartment, Maunders dismissed the attending lackey and prepared to put his master to bed.

This task, however, proved more than Maunders had expected, for his drunken master would insist on acting as one dead, therefore rendering it necessary for the servant to once again employ the aid of the porter, this time to remove his master's clothes. Stefan snored loudly as they finally got him abed and, after a despairing look, the two servants beat a weary retreat, leaving him to sleep off the effects of what they termed the "blue ruin."

CHAPTER THREE

It was almost noon the following morning when Stefan finally made his way down to the breakfast parlor, where the duke had long finished his early repast but remained, reading the morning journal. Noting Stefan wince as the door closed behind him, his grace eyed his cousin with some mockery. "Had a good night, coz?" he inquired, grinning.

"Can't remember much about it," Stefan confessed, drawing a chair away from the table and slumping heavily into it. "All I can remember is that we are expected at Markham's home sometime tomorrow. The fellow has invited us to stay."

"The deuce he has," growled his grace, showing no small signs of annoyance. "I take it, then, that we are to spend Christmas under his roof. A plan that does not exactly fire me with enthusiasm. I trust you conveyed our heartfelt thanks for the generous invitation?"

"Oh, take a damper, Marcel," replied Stefan, frowning heavily and placing a shaking hand on his thundering brow. "Don't you think I tried to put him off the idea, but he would insist on us going? It's only for three days, and I'm sure we can survive that long. Besides, rumor has it that his eldest daughter has just come over from England, so there should prove some interest in that direction. I've heard she's a regular little beauty."

Vaguely, the name Julie Markham tugged at the duke's memory, but the interlude had been so brief that it had made no lasting impression; therefore, he made not the connection and put it aside. Instead, pouring out two cups of coffee, he said, "Not my type of woman. It's not my usual practice to enter into a flirtation with innocent and dull females, and certainly not in their own home!"

"May I once more remind you that women are not to be put into *types?*" grinned Stefan, not without some effort as the thudding in his head reached a crescendo. "I guarantee that if she is half as beautiful as one is led to believe, she will have you in her toils long before our stay is over."

"You might find the thought appealing,"

drawled his grace, drawing his chair away from the table and going to sit by the fire. "However, I have yet to see a female of impeccable upbringing who will hold any attraction for me."

"Quite so," countered Stefan with a knowing smile, "but we will argue no further on that head."

"Argue?" replied his grace in mock amazement. "My dear Stefan, I am never known to argue. We merely discuss a point on which we differ. I can assure you, I have no wish to contradict my host, especially as you have been so kind as to put a roof over my head!"

Stefan gave a reluctant chuckle. "Devil take you. You know I'm devilishly glad to have you here."

"Yes," agreed his grace, "as you so frequently feel the need to tell me. I am also devilishly glad to be here. Now, that exhausts that topic!"

Stefan gave a shout of laughter but, once more feeling the effects of his hangover, he pressed a shaking hand to his brow, muttering a severe oath. "Should never drink home brew," he confided. "Never know what they put in the stuff."

Rising and lazily stretching his arms, the duke stirred the fire with an elegantly booted foot. "I know the very thing for you," he said. "I'm a firm believer in the 'hair of the dog,' and although you don't possess any home brew, I am sure claret will serve the purpose admirably." So saying, he crossed to a small table in a recess by the window, where a decanter and glasses stood on a silver tray and, after measuring out two glasses and proffering one to Stefan, returned to his seat by the fire.

"Know what I think?" said Stefan over the rim of his glass.

"No, pray enlighten me," replied his grace, toying with his quizzing glass and marveling as to what proportions it magnified his emerald ring.

"I think you are getting soft, Marcel."

The duke's countenance visibly darkened, but he replied lightly, "My dear Stefan, whatever gave you that idea?"

"Never known you to turn tail and run before. I mean, not like you not to face the consequences."

"What the devil are you talking about?" said his grace with considerable asperity.

"The duel!"

"I did not *turn tail and run,* as you phrase it. I was obliged to keep our family name free from any further scandal. I have to establish my sister creditably, and Lord

Strafford reminded me of my obligations to her. He would have been obliged to withdraw his suit had our fair name once more been dragged through the mire. As it is, my flight to Paris enables the matter to be settled out of hand."

"Never known you to be bothered about public opinion before," said Stefan, steadfastly regarding his cousin's profile. "Fact is, as you've told me the story, I'm inclined to think the young pup got his true desserts. So why did you run?"

"Perhaps you have the right of it, after all," replied the duke. "Perhaps I am going soft, even entering my dotage, but the thought of scandal does not appeal as it once did."

"Thought you were," said Stefan with conviction.

"Thought I was what?"

"Getting soft. Bats in your belfry, if you ask me."

"My dear cousin," said his grace in deceptively sweet tones, "if you don't let the matter rest, I'm afraid I will be obliged to serve you with a display of fisticuffs, which, although fatiguing, will be quite necessary if you persist in your present strain of conversation. I have the reputation of having a notable left and of being able to plant a good facer. So in the terms of the pugilist, if you don't wish me to draw your cork, *taises vous.*"

"Just so," agreed Stefan, hastily drawing his chair away from the table. "Knew you were not really soft, but just in case you should still entertain the idea of drawing my cork, I will relieve you of my presence."

"An estimable idea. Pray do not let me detain you," answered the duke thunderously, so darkly, in fact, that Stefan lost no time in making good his retreat.

His grace sat meditatively gazing into the fire, slowly sipping his claret before finally deciding to go to Gaultier's, which opened its doors to likeminded individuals from noon. It would appear he had not been in the most pleasant of moods for quite some time, a fact that he attributed to boredom with the whole of society. He realized that his entire lifestyle did not hold the attraction it once had, and he became firm in his belief that he was suffering from a case of ennui, symptoms of which, it seemed, not even the lures of Paris could cure.

When the duke and his cousin met over supper that evening, nothing more was said of the duel, but Stefan, finding some restraint in the duke's manner, was moved to apologize for anything he might have said under the influence of a hangover.

The drive to Sefron Towers lasted a little above two hours, the while of which his grace and Stefan played a hand or two of piquet. Oakes and Stefan's valet followed in a second coach, each jealously guarding his master's portmanteau. Neither of the two cousins was looking forward to the coming visit, but when the chaise finally swept up the drive of his lordship's house, they each had to admit that it was certainly an impressive building. It stood some four stories high, with a covered porch leading to large oak doors framed by marble pillars. Ivy rambled over the walls up to the third-story windows, giving it an air of old England. The grounds in which Sefron stood would be magnificent in spring. Even the wintry blast could not detract from its settings. Lawns stretched down to flower beds at the end of which was a stone balustrade and then lawns and shrubs on a slightly lower level, resembling something of an Italian setting.

Almost as soon as the chaise was halted before the large stone steps of the porch, Lord Markham appeared in the doorway, his stocky figure well framed by the oaken doors. Stefan was the first to alight, and at sight of him his lordship lost no time in hurrying forward, hand extended in a warm greeting.

"Stefan, my boy," he said and beamed. "Welcome to my humble abode. Ah, Lear, so glad to see you. Come in, come in. I'm sure the both of you could do with a drop of brandy and the warmth of a good blaze after your drive."

The visitors accepted his offer by a slight inclination of the head and followed his lordship into the large hall, from which a wide staircase swept, giving access to the ornate galleries of the first and second landings.

A lackey preceded his master and held open a door at the rear of the hall, and his lordship bade them enter the library. "This is my only retreat," he said, bidding them to be seated. "I find that my wife and daughters are busy organizing everything for tonight's ball, only a small affair don't you know, and this is the only room as yet left unmolested. If you will but excuse me for a moment, I will tell my wife that you have arrived. The festivities don't start until this evening, so you may be perfectly at your ease." At this, he bustled out of the room to find her ladyship, who was engaged below stairs, presiding over the whole with quiet confidence.

"I don't think it will be as boring as we expected," said Stefan, draining his glass.

"We haven't met her ladyship yet," mused his grace, slowly swinging a well-booted leg to and fro as he sat on the arm of a chair. "She's probably one of those old matrons perpetually living in the past and forever regaling anyone who will listen about the day she was presented at court."

"What of the daughter?" asked Stefan, refilling his glass and raising it in a silent toast.

"She is to be seen to be believed," said the duke. "In all probability, she is a spoiled beauty who has a fit of the vapors whenever her will is crossed."

"You judge us too harshly," snapped an indignant voice from the doorway. "Spoiled I may be, but I am not so poor spirited as to have the vapors, and neither is Mama an old matron who goes on for hours about court life."

Both Stefan and the duke leaped to their feet, staring guiltily at the slender figure of a girl standing just a little way into the room. Stefan was the first to find his power of speech. "Ma'am, we most humbly beg your pardon," he stammered, executing a deep bow. "We had no idea . . ."

"Obviously not!" she said, advancing farther into the room with a crispness to her step and a swish of blue satin skirts. She was enticingly petite, with slender hands that were now clasped before her. Dusky ringlets framed a face that was delicately tinged with color, and large blue eyes scrutinized the cousins as they stood before her.

"Is it not usual to reserve judgment until you have met those in question?" she asked, her usually pleasantly low voice shaking with righteous indignation.

"Quite so," agreed his grace languidly, stepping forward to meet her and proffering a brief bow. "Our profound apologies. We have heard of your beauty, but naught of your temperament. Yes, a little spoiled I think, but certainly not poor spirited. If your mama is anything like you, I'm sure our stay will be everything that is amiable."

"It seems that I must revise my first opinion of you, your grace," she said. "I find you even more insufferable than when we first met. That I could overlook, but now I find you intolerable!"

"Yes, we have met before," replied his grace thoughtfully, allowing his gaze to run over her. "Though it is quite remiss of me, I fear I have no memory of the encounter.

Could it be that we have met at court?"

"It was Dieppe, sir. Is your memory so short?"

"Dieppe?"

"You were so obliging as to allow me one of your rooms at the inn."

"Ah, yes, Miss Julie Markham, the girl with the smiling eyes, and one who will not be aided by strangers. I made no connection. Yes, I remember now. I'm afraid you subjected me to excessive discomfort. Oakes, my valet, snores, and he kept me awake nearly half the night."

"That I am quite sure he did not," replied Julie with some asperity. "Anyone who lacks all sensibility, as you so obviously do, could sleep through anything."

"Come, ma'am, let us cry truce," chuckled the duke, extending his hand. "A battle of wits is far too tiring at this hour of the day, and it is not my wish to incur your wrath so early in my visit."

"I never have a battle of wits with my father's guests," she answered, ignoring the outstretched hand. "I hope your stay will be everything that is pleasant," and she turned as if to leave.

"There is nothing more certain," said his grace, a decided twinkle in his eye. "I will endeavor to make my stay not wholly abhorrent in your sight, my dear."

"Pray do not put yourself out on my account, sir," she answered, turning once more to face the cousins and dropping a mock curtsy.

"I never put myself out unless it suits me," he countered smoothly. "Dare I hope that you will reserve a dance for me at the ball this evening?"

"I'm afraid I am committed for the whole evening, your grace," Julie replied, meeting his gaze defiantly. "However, I am sure there will be many other mademoiselles who would be honored by your attentions."

He feigned disappointment but was unable to disguise the amusement in his voice. "Alas, I have no heart to dance with another." His interest was piqued. Perhaps his stay would be quite entertaining after all.

"I will leave you to pine then, sir," she replied, retreating to the door before the duke could see the responsive gleam she was unable to hide.

CHAPTER FOUR

Lady Markham was not at all as the duke had predicted. She was a small, motherly person who made all haste to make the two cousins feel at home, and later that evening, when the other guests arrived, she proved to be an invaluable hostess.

From the security of her father's side, Julie watched the duke descend the grand staircase. Unwillingly fascinated by this arrogant yet strikingly handsome man, she continued to monitor his progress into the crowded ballroom, noting his elegant dress and assurance of manner. He had not left her thoughts since his arrival earlier in the day, and she had alternated between an overwhelming desire to see him humbled and an irrepressible wish to learn more of him.

Oblivious to such interest, Marcel stood just within the portals of the ballroom, obviously seeking his cousin. He had honored the occasion of the ball by wearing his new ensemble from Sternhill's and was the envy of several young blades as he made his way among the guests, pausing here and there to acknowledge various acquaintances. His coat was of midnight velvet, with satin knee breeches to match, and he wore a waistcoat of silver brocade. Sapphires and diamonds twinkled as so many stars in the foaming white lace at his throat and also on his shoes and hair buckle. Alas, to Oakes' despair, the duke had bade his valet to put away the hare's foot and rouge and refused the blue hair powder, favoring instead the white. A large signet ring adorned his left hand, but his right, which held a gold snuffbox, was innocent of further jewels.

Lord Markham had said that it was only to be a small affair but, to the duke's experienced eye, there seemed to be at least a hundred couples in the large ballroom. Silks, velvets, and lace all flowed together in an endless stream of color while hundreds of candles burned brightly overhead in shimmering chandeliers and glass sconces. Lackeys in black-and-gold livery hovered at strategic points to attend to the guests' every need, while a quintet played the first movements of a quadrille.

Entering the refreshment room, he spied

Stefan procuring a glass of Madeira for a rather sour-faced dowager and, deeming it wise to rescue his cousin from such an unkind fate, extricated him from the lady's side. Much to the duke's disgust, Stefan seemed a trifle foxed already. Not so much as to make it obvious, but enough for him to be slightly slurring his speech.

"I've stolen a march on you, Marcel," he announced, thankfully clutching the duke's arm. "Just been talking with Miss Markham, and I've engaged her for one of the supper dances. Not bad, eh?"

"Very clever of you," agreed his grace, taking no apparent interest in the issue.

"Thought you'd say that," replied Stefan, beaming at his own ingeniousness.

"Am I so predictable?" drawled the duke. "I must change my mode of address."

"Don't be so damned sardonic," snapped Stefan. "It won't wash with me. I've known you too long."

"My dear coz," said his grace, taking Stefan's arm in a viselike grip, "if you are trying to pick a quarrel with me, I'll have none of it."

As Stefan appeared decidedly unsteady, the duke thrust him into a nearby chair, ordering him to remain there until he had more command of his senses.

Just as the duke left his cousin, Lady Markham appeared at his side. She looked most elegant in a dress of burgundy velvet laced with gold, cut wide at the bodice and spread over large panniers.

"I'm afraid you have not been dancing, your grace," she said, taking his arm. "Pray allow me to find a suitable partner for you. Yes, I think I have the very one in mind. She is Monsieur Badeau's daughter and is such a sweet child. Come, I will make the necessary introductions."

Resigned to his fate, the duke followed her ladyship and it was with an air of bored tolerance that he led out Mlle. Therese Badeau. While he found her a pleasing enough partner, he had no desire to further the acquaintance, and therefore it was with no reluctance that at the end of the set he gave her up to Bertram, the oldest of Lord Markham's four sons.

As his grace stood discoursing with Lord Trent, an old friend, he found himself watching Julie as she made her way down a set of the gavotte on the arm of an elderly gallant. She was dressed in white crystal satin over an underskirt of silver, with a single silver rose at her waist. Her hair was dressed à la Pompadour and lightly powdered, with a diamond clasp confining her ringlets to one side, while a single diamond lay suspended on a gold chain around her neck. A very pleasing sight, thought the duke, returning his attention to Lord Trent but still keeping a watchful eye on the dancers.

It was thus that Stefan found his cousin as he staggered across the room, holding a shaking hand to his brow.

"I fear my head is about to split, Marcel," he said in muffled tones. "I'm in need of assistance. Would you lend me your arm, as I fear I will not make my chamber unaided? Make my apologies to Miss Markham. I find I am unable to stand up with her for the supper dance."

"I don't know why you bother to drink," said the duke harshly, taking hold of his arm and propelling him out of the ballroom and up the staircase. "You know you have no head for it, and all you do is make a fool of yourself. Get your man to prepare a brew. Perhaps that will sober you."

Stefan submitted silently to the duke's reproof and allowed himself to be thrust into his room without further ado, collapsing gratefully onto the large four-poster bed, eyes closed, appearing almost dead to the world.

His grace returned to the ballroom just as

the supper dances began and spied Julie talking with Lord and Lady Markham at the farther end of the room. Making his leisurely way toward the family group, he prepared to present Stefan's apologies.

"Again I find you not dancing, your grace," chided Lady Markham as the duke bowed low over her hand. "I fear you may not be finding our ball entertaining."

"On the contrary, madam, I find it *fort amusant*," he said, smiling. Turning to Julie, he made a profound leg. "Miss Markham, I hope you will forgive me, but I am sent with a message from my cousin. He offers his deepest regrets, but he finds himself slightly indisposed and is unable to stand up with you for the supper dance."

"It is of no consequence, your grace," replied Julie, obviously still smarting from their previous encounter. "One is obliged to make allowances for one's guests. I only hope that he will not suffer too severely from his *indisposition* in the morning!"

"Julie!" remonstrated her ladyship sharply. "That is no way to answer his grace. Apologize immediately."

"You are quite right, Mama," relented Julie. "Forgive me, your grace. I did not mean to seem so disagreeable."

He chuckled, bowing briefly. "There is

nothing to forgive, Miss Markham," he said with a teasing light in his eyes. "May I therefore offer myself as a suitable partner in his stead?"

Piqued at his obvious amusement, Julie tilted her chin defiantly. "There must be far more willing partners than I, your grace —"

"Nonsense, me gal," bellowed his lordship, embarrassed at his daughter's uncivil refusal. "I won't have you standing around like a peagoose. Dance with the man!"

His countenance alight with amusement, the duke inclined his head toward his host, saying, "My thanks, Markham." It was not usual that any partner of his choosing should appear reluctant, and he found it somewhat of a novelty. This young girl was definitely an original, quite out of the ordinary. At her father's instigation, however, Julie laid her hand lightly on his proffered arm and allowed him to lead her onto the floor to join the waiting set. Taking her left hand in his clasp, he waited for the orchestra to begin the minuet. Julie was a natural dancer, but for some reason she felt nervous and for several movements appeared preoccupied with her steps, and she answered his grace very much at random. Being so much shorter than the duke, her head only just reached above his shoulder, and when the movement of the dance brought them together she felt an unexpected shyness and did not look up but steadfastly regarded his lace cravat.

The Duke of Lear, who was not in the habit of devoting his time to young, inexperienced ladies, found this shyness somewhat amusing and not altogether unattractive. Had he been a younger man, he reflected, he would have succumbed to her charm. It was fortunate, however, that he was nine and twenty and well past the age to be caught by a pretty face and naïve ways. He reminded himself that naïveté was not what he looked for in a female companion and knew he would tire of it sooner or later, as he had of so many other unique charms. For had not experience taught him that rarely did a superior mind go hand in hand with a beautiful face and that beauty alone only held an attraction until one's own mind demanded more?

"It is a very interesting cravat, is it not, Miss Markham?" he asked quizzically. That did make her look up, her face breaking into a smile. Her eyes met his with such a frank, ingenuous expression in their depths that he was taken quite off guard and became aware of a stirring of something in his breast that was not wholly amusement.

70

"I beg your pardon, your grace," she said and smiled, "but I was minding my steps."

"A very worthwhile occupation, I am sure," agreed the duke, "but one I hardly think necessary, for you dance delightfully, my dear."

Julie blushed delicately and returned to contemplating the cravat.

His grace gave a soft laugh. "Come, Julie, don't be shy with me," he coaxed.

"I don't remember making you free to use my name, sir," she said, looking up with what she hoped would be a scornful glance but not wholly managing to suppress some amusement.

"Then make me free, for whether you give me leave or not, I shall use it. Come, can we not be friends? Did I not relinquish a bedchamber to you and suffer damnably as a result? I am not such a terrible ogre. At least, I think not. I have not eaten any maidens for at least a sennight. That's better," he said with approval as Julie gave a reluctant chuckle. "I'm sure we will deal famously. Indeed, you are far prettier when you smile."

"I am not smiling," she lied, valiantly trying not to before finally relenting and admitting to herself that she found his charm impossible to withstand.

"Devil take this dance," said the duke good-humoredly, as they were surrounded by the press of couples. "I think we would be better going in search of refreshments. I vow I would rather talk to you than dance on a milling floor."

"But, sir," said Julie, mischievously peeping up through lowered lashes, "did you not engage to stand up with me for a supper dance?"

"My dear, you are in need of negus," he purred, relentlessly leading her from the floor.

"Am I?" she rebelled, feigning reluctance.

"I believe that you are!"

"But I am not in the least thirsty, sir."

The duke laughed and, making a deep bow, he raised her hand to his lips. "My dear Miss Markham, pray allow me to refresh you with a glass of negus."

"My very need, sir," she said and smiled, dropping a slight curtsy and allowing him to guide her from the room.

The supper room was full to overflowing, and it was some minutes before his grace found a suitable table, but this eventually achieved, he bade the attending lackey to bring the necessary sustenance in the form of two glasses of negus and a plate of sweet-meats.

"I would have thought that you would prefer a glass of claret or burgundy," said Julie, watching with some amusement his noble attempt to drink his negus unflinchingly.

"I make it a rule never to drink when I am with a lady," he replied, putting aside the distasteful liquid.

Julie gave a gurgle of laughter and said, "Sir, I have four brothers, so it would be nothing to me to see a glass of wine on the table. Please, instead of suffering for my sake, allow a lackey to fetch you something more to your liking."

"Thank you, but no," he replied, staying firm to his resolve, and then, seeing a large, pompous gallant approach: "I am afraid, my dear, that it would seem that I am about to lose you to the superior charms of the Marquis de Coustellet, who, unless I am mistaken, is fastly bearing down upon us, intent on claiming you for the next dance."

Marcel rose at the gentleman's approach as if to leave, but Julie nervously caught his sleeve, saying in urgent undertones, "Please, sir, don't go."

Hearing this faint plea with some mild astonishment, the duke obediently stood behind her chair and greeted Coustellet with a cold civility. Likewise, to the duke's surprise, did Julie, favoring the unfortunate gallant with only the briefest of nods.

"Your obedient, Lear," said Coustellet silkily. "Your very slave, Mademoiselle Markham. I have come to claim you for the next country dance, my fair butterfly. My entire happiness depends upon you this night."

"I am afraid you come too late, sir," said Julie, slightly drawing into her seat. "I am already promised to his grace."

"But I am sure Lear will be only too glad to relinquish his claim at one word from you, my rose."

The duke, encountering a pleading look from Julie and rightfully interpreting it, turned scornfully upon Coustellet.

"That, *mon ami,* is where you are quite mistaken," he said, at his most haughty. "I have no intention of relinquishing anything for your gratification, least of all Miss Markham. I therefore hope you will excuse us if we return to the ballroom."

For a moment the two men stood looking at each other, Coustellet, his hand going automatically for the sword he was not wearing. The duke, infuriatingly at ease, lazily toyed with his quizzing glass, a slow sardonic smile crossing his countenance at the marquis' discomfiture.

"It will be as you wish, Lear," seethed Coustellet, his already florid countenance suffusing with color. "I bow to your ruling for this night, but there will be another time." And then turning to Julie: "I hope I will have the honor of escorting you to the hunt on the twenty-sixth, *ma chère.* That pleasure I am sure you cannot deny me."

Julie gave a mumbled reply to this and, rising, took her leave on the duke's arm, leaving Coustellet to seethe alone.

"Thank you, your grace," she whispered as soon as they were out of hearing, her hand plucking nervously at the duke's velvet cuff. "I don't know why, but I hate that man. He frightens me."

"He is not the pleasantest of men," agreed the duke, patting her hand reassuringly. "I myself have no great liking for him. His boorish manner does not exactly endear him to society. But come, we turn melancholy. We will not let him spoil our enjoyment. You avowed that you were promised to me for the next country dance, and now I will hold you to that promise."

With a gurgle of laughter, Julie regained some of her former gaiety and allowed the duke to lead her into the set then forming, her steps perfectly matching his as they traversed the floor.

The evening flew by, and when it came to an end Julie was not the only one regretting its termination, for it had been many a month since the Duke of Lear had so thoroughly enjoyed a ball — or any other amusement, if truth were told. Oakes, who had been waiting up for his master, was quite surprised at the duke's cheerfulness; he even went so far as to say that his grace was actually humming a tune, which, although almost unrecognizable, proved that he was well pleased.

CHAPTER FIVE

A sharp frost heralded the dawn of Christmas Day, and after breakfasting late in his chamber, the Duke of Lear joined his cousin in the morning room, where members of the Markham family were eagerly exchanging gifts.

At first, the duke held himself aloof from the gathering but, to his surprise, far from feeling bored, he found that he was actually enjoying the informality of the occasion. It had been so long since he had participated in a family Christmas that he had forgotten just how pleasant such events could be. He was completely taken aback, however, when three-year-old Sally, the youngest member of the Markham family, approached and demanded that he examine her gifts. After an astonished moment, he gave way to a sudden whim and allowed the child to lay all before him. Indeed, anyone in the know would not have recognized my lord duke, so far was he departed from his usual haughty manner.

Wholly oblivious to formality, Sally tugged unceremoniously at the skirts of the duke's black velvet coat whenever she thought him not to be paying the required attention. Her little face glowed with happiness, and her dark corkscrew curls bobbed about as she did a little jig for his edification.

"Knee," she demanded unceremoniously of the duke, who, quite at a loss as to her meaning, allowed her to scramble unchallenged onto his lap. Just at that moment, Stefan strolled up looking somewhat amused.

"Why, Marcel," he said and grinned, "knew you had a fatal fascination for the fairer sex, but must you charm young ladies of such tender years who are not yet out of the nursery? You have no idea just how comical you look. Strap me if you don't look absolutely terrified of the poor mite."

"A very astute summary of the situation," admitted his grace ruefully. "Just what exactly does one do with these, er — little ladies? I'm afraid I am quite at a loss as to what is expected of me. She seems to think my quizzing glass some kind of sweetmeat and will insist on sucking it!" True enough, Sally sat happily on the duke's knee, fascinated by the aforesaid object.

"I say, Marcel, you mustn't let her eat it," exclaimed Stefan, as much at a loss as his cousin as to what to do with this young temptress. "I mean, hardly the thing. Why don't you take her to her mama?"

His grace was just about to comply when Sally threw her arms unconcernedly around his neck and planted a rather sticky kiss on his cheek. "You pretty gentlepum," she announced, which had the effect of confounding her gallant and sending Stefan into whoops of unholy mirth.

"That's a good one," he said amidst gales of laughter. "Hey, Sally, don't you think I'm pretty?"

"No," was the dampening reply as she hunted unchallenged in the duke's capacious pockets, but as they yielded only a lace handkerchief, she took to contemplating his rings. Her rather quelling answer had the effect of making Stefan strive to draw her away from his cousin, as Stefan never refused a challenge when a lady's affections were concerned. It then became a battle between the two to amuse her, but Sally, keeping faithful to her first love, pushed Stefan away and bestowed yet another kiss upon the duke.

The two cousins, although complete

amateurs, managed to keep the youngest Miss Markham thoroughly amused, and so engrossed were they in their task that they failed to notice Julie observing them from where she sat in conversation with Bertram. Upon perceiving her little sister attempting to untie the duke's lace cravat, she deemed it time Sally was taken back to the nursery.

The remainder of the day passed pleasantly, the duke astonishing his cousin by actually playing at lottery tickets with Julie and her two other sisters: Anne, aged twelve, and Sophie, sixteen. It was not, however, until the next day that his grace saw Julie alone.

Everyone had gone to the hunt excepting Julie, who had pleaded a headache; Lady Markham, who never rode to hounds; and his grace, for whom fox hunting in France held no interest.

It was about half an hour before midday when his grace, about to enter the library, heard a scuffle and a muffled cry come from the drawing room and, vaguely interested in its source, languidly opened the drawing room door. The scene that met his gaze, however, cast aside all languor. Julie was found to be struggling in Coustellet's passionate embrace, most obviously repulsed by his amorous attentions and vainly attempting to free herself from his hold. Coustellet, having his back to the door, neither saw nor heard the duke's entrance, and it was with no mild surprise that he felt his collar taken in a strangling grip and himself thrown bodily to the floor.

After briefly asserting that Julie was unhurt, Marcel wrenched Coustellet to his feet and drove his fist into his jaw. Staggering back, Coustellet shook his head before rushing forward like an enraged bull. Throwing a wild right, he caught the point of the duke's jaw, but a follow-up to this move was confused by his grace serving Coustellet a heavy blow to the chest, which felled him to the ground. Again Coustellet was on his feet, and this time he was favored with a lucky punch that drew a spattering of blood from the duke's nose. The thrashing that his grace then administered to the unfortunate gallant was suddenly cut short by Coustellet who, finding himself once more companion to the floor, in desperation grabbed a nearby footstool and, quickly rising, dealt his grace a foul blow to the side of his head.

Marcel sank semiconscious to his knees while Coustellet, taking full advantage of the situation, ran to the open casement by which he had entered and beat a hasty

81

retreat in the direction of the stables.

Julie ran stumbling forward to help the duke who, having risen rather shakily to his feet, was gingerly feeling the swelling that was fast forming over his left temple. He managed, however, to execute a graceful, if somewhat short, bow. "You must forgive me, my dear," he said, succumbing to Julie's ministrations and sitting in a large chair. "It was not my wish that you should be witness to such a vulgar turn of fisticuffs, especially one in which I should suffer the indignity of being defeated by a footstool!"

There had been a light of amusement in the duke's eye as he spoke these last few words, and Julie could not help but give a reluctant chuckle. "It was neat, was it not?" she agreed. "If only Bertram could have seen you, he would be your eternal friend. There's nothing he likes better than a mill."

"In that case, perhaps I should repeat the whole performance for his edification," said the duke, with an attempt at levity. Seeing that her hand trembled, he took her fingers in his warm clasp, his gaze intent on her face. "Did he hurt you?" he asked quietly.

"Apart from a few cracked ribs, I think not," she said in an attempt to mirror his flippancy. She tentatively raised her finger to the bruise that was spreading at his temple. "It is you who are hurt, sir, and all for my sake. I do beg your pardon. Coustellet entered unannounced and took me by surprise. I had thought him at the hunt with the others but, upon finding me absent, he came back to Sefron, supposing me to be alone." Julie's eyes fell before the duke's fiery scrutiny. "And — and then he tried to force his attentions on me," she stammered, unable to hide her distress at the situation. Then she whispered, with a catch in her voice, "I don't know what I would have done if you had not intervened."

"Probably used the footstool on him," replied the duke with a lightness he was far from feeling. Then, unable to disguise his anger any longer: "I shall find it necessary to pay our amorous friend a visit in the very near future, so if you would be so kind as to furnish me with his direction . . ."

"No!" she cried hotly. Then, as the duke looked sharply at her, she said, a little more calmly, "I will not allow you to be put out on my account, sir."

"I think Coustellet has already *put me out,* as you term it," purred the duke at his most unpleasant. "There is now an issue between us that must be settled. His actions toward you cannot be allowed to go unpunished."

"But it must go no further," she persisted.

"No one must know, not even my father, who holds Coustellet in strong aversion. It would be said that I encouraged him by staying away from the hunt, apparently alone." Her gaze swept his face and, as if suddenly becoming aware that his fingers still held hers, she pulled her hand away, saying, "Where are my senses? Your head must ache terribly, and there is a very large bruise fast appearing."

"You need not worry," said the duke, making to rise.

Julie gently but firmly pressed him back into the chair. "I will get you something for the swelling," she said, and without waiting for an answer hurried from the room.

His grace was not very much hurt, but of a sudden he had taken a liking to being pampered and allowed Julie, when she returned, to bathe his temple with a cooling lotion. She perched herself on the arm of his chair, requiring him to hold a small china bowl wherein reposed the soothing liquid, and gently bathed the offending lump.

The duke, deeming it prudent not to mention Coustellet, in an attempt to divert her thoughts asked lightly, "Did you enjoy your season in London?"

Julie smiled ruefully, thankful for the

diversion. "I'm afraid my aunt, who was to have brought me out, suffered a seizure just before the season began, and so my debut had to be postponed. However, Papa has promised that I will have a season next year."

"No doubt your debut will be a great success, my dear," the duke said, smiling. "Indeed, it is an event I shall look forward to with great anticipation."

As Julie gently smiled in response, he involuntarily became fascinated by the turn of her delicate cheek and for the moment imagined his lips resting there. Mentally taking himself to task, he attempted to banish such errant thoughts, but against his will the fascination remained. When, inadvertently spilling some of the liquid on his coat, Julie leaned closer to his profile in an attempt to dab away the offending liquid, he found the temptation impossible to resist. Without conscious thought, he gently tilted up her chin and tenderly kissed the sweet roundness of her face.

For a moment she gazed blankly at him, and then with a sudden cry she ran from the room and up to her apartments, locking her door against all intruders, and there she spent the remainder of the day.

The Duke of Lear, cursing himself for being every type of fool, reflected that he had treated her hardly better than Coustellet by taking advantage of her trusting innocence. It had, however, taken him completely by surprise that he could feel so tenderly toward her, for he had thought himself impervious to her charms, and it was in some consternation that he also retired to his room.

Although situated in the country, Sefron Towers kept town hours and served supper at eight. About half an hour before this time, Stefan knocked on his cousin's dressing room door and, upon being granted admission, entered just as the duke dismissed Oakes.

"Had a good run?" inquired the duke, putting the finishing touches to his cravat.

"Devilishly slow to start," replied Stefan, perching himself on the arm of a chair, "but we put a rare 'un up about noon, and he gave us a four-mile run. Hey, I say, coz, what's happened to your head? You've got the deuce of a lump."

Marcel grimaced ruefully. "That is a fact of which I am painfully aware. I walked into the library door."

Stefan laughed derisively. "Nonsense, that won't fadge! Walked into a door, my foot!

Looks more like a mill to me, though I never thought anyone could plant you a facer. Must have had a fist of iron."

"No, just a footstool," replied the duke under his breath.

"Eh?" said Stefan stupidly.

"Nothing," replied the duke, laughing. "I walked into the door, that is all."

"Well, I don't like that story above half. You'll catch cold telling that one, Marcel, but if you've no mind to tell me more, I'll not force your hand." Then hopefully: "Don't suppose you'd like to tell me the truth though, would you?"

"No, I would not," agreed the duke. "You can help me, though, by repeating my story if you are asked, but without the embellishment of any of your own notions."

"There's something harvy-carvy going on, but I won't press my point. If that's your story, I'll stick to it."

Stefan was on the point of departure when he suddenly turned from the door. "My wits seem to have gone a-begging, coz," he said, returning once more. "Markham's asked us to stay for a couple of weeks hunting. I thought I'd better ask you before committing us. Everyone else is leaving tomorrow, but he thinks we might enjoy hunting with his new pack. He's got a new horse for you to try, a real prime piece of flesh, or so he tells me. About sixteen hands high, good breadth of chest, strong quarters, length of neck — everything as it should be. Have you a mind to it? Do we stay?"

"As we have no further engagements, it may prove entertaining," drawled the duke. "You may inform his lordship that we accept his invitation."

"On your high ropes, ain't you, coz?" reproved Stefan, unsure of his companion's mood.

The duke turned toward him, his countenance schooled to one of innocence. "A fact of which I was unaware," he said contritely. "It would seem I must beg your pardon."

"Damn you, you always were sardonic," laughed Stefan, "but if you have a mind to stay, I've no objections. I'm enjoying myself. That Julie's a great girl, is she not?"

"Um," replied his grace pensively.

"Ho, got you in her toils, has she?"

"My dear Stefan, she is a mere child."

"She's no child — almost twenty. She's a woman, Marcel."

"Perhaps you have the right of it," mused his grace, gazing abstractly into the fire while his thoughts roamed elsewhere.

Stefan cast his cousin a wry look, saying, "So, that's the way the wind blows. Well, I wish you luck, Marcel."

To this, his grace vouched no answer.

Stefan was true to his word when, a short while later, Lord Markham and his company took their places at the supper table. Everyone in turn exclaimed and laughed at the duke's mishap, but both cousins stayed firm to the fabrication, only the duke winced slightly to think that they should believe him such a ready fool as to walk into a door. He was well repaid, however, by a grateful look from Julie, who, sitting opposite him, hardly glanced up from her plate all through the meal.

The repast over, the ladies retired to the sitting room and the gentlemen sat over their port, relating over and over again how Stefan had ridden his horse at a large stone wall and ditch without the slightest hesitation during the hunt that morning, greatly disconcerting Stefan, who disclaimed such a foolhardy action.

Upon joining the ladies, his grace noted that Julie was not among the company, and so, intent on apologizing, he inquired of her whereabouts of a lackey at that moment employed in erecting the card tables for a quiet game of Silver Loo. The lackey believed mademoiselle to be alone in the library, to whence repaired the duke immediately.

Despite receiving no answer to his knock, his grace entered and stood for a moment on the threshold, surveying the scene. The candles had not been lit, but a large log fire burning in the grate fitfully illuminated the figure of a girl reposing on the couch. The duke thought her to be asleep and, laying his hand on the door handle, he prepared to take his leave, but something stayed him. At first he thought he was mistaken, but upon hearing it again, he realized that Julie was sobbing. In an instant he was kneeling beside her and, perceiving him, she hastily sat up, ineffectually trying to hide her tears.

"My dear girl, have I given you such a dislike of me?" he asked softly. "I most humbly beg your forgiveness. I — I was a fool!"

"No, no, it is not that," replied Julie, fighting hard against her tears. "I, too, behaved foolishly."

The duke was visibly relieved and, taking her hand, whispered, "Then what is it, chéri?"

"He's dead," she sobbed, withdrawing her hand from his clasp.

"Who?" he asked gently.

"Jasper."

"I do not know Jasper."

"He was my dog."

"Your dog?"

Again the sobs wracked her slight frame as she nodded, unable to speak.

For just a moment, his grace knew an impulse to catch her to him but, reluctant to lose favor with her, with great fortitude resisted the desire. Previously, a sobbing female would have sent him hot-foot for the door but, inexplicably, he knew only the desire to comfort her. Her obvious distress served only to strengthen his resolve, and, as Julie's sobs showed no signs of abating, he threw caution to the wind. Sitting beside her, he gently drew her head onto his shoulder. She clutched gratefully at his coat, weeping unrestrainedly for several minutes, and then, as her tears began to subside, she realized the impropriety of her position and made a move to sit up. He would have kept her within the circle of his arm a moment longer but, realizing the dangers of this, made no attempt to retain her.

"I must beg your grace's pardon —" she began, ineffectually dabbing at her eyes with a very damp handkerchief.

"There is absolutely no need," broke in the duke. "The dog was dear to you. I quite understand." Producing his own handkerchief, he proceeded to wipe away her tears.

"He was missing all day," she explained haltingly, hiccupping on sobs. "Then just after supper the kennel man came to tell me that they had found him about a mile away with his leg broken and they had had to shoot him." For a moment it seemed as though she was going to weep again, but then she continued. "Apparently, Jasper must have set out after the hounds this morning but lost their trail and took the wrong direction. They found him in the quarry."

"These things happen, *chéri*. It was an accident and could not be avoided," said the duke softly. "You will feel his loss most keenly, but be comforted that he is out of pain now, and that is what you would wish, is it not?"

"Yes."

"Come then, dry your tears before you cry yourself into a headache. You must go up to bed now. Everything will seem a deal better in the morning."

Obediently, Julie rose to go and, after a brief *bonne nuit,* left the duke to seek the comfort of her chamber.

For a moment, his grace sat deep in thought, and then, as the clock chimed the hour, he roused himself from his musings and made his way to his apartment. Here the faithful Oakes awaited his master's orders in the dressing room and upon receiving a summons from the duke hurried to assist him to undress.

It was not, however, for this office that he was needed. His grace, waving aside Oakes' would-be ministrations, said in his languid way, "At first light, I require you to leave for England, Oakes."

"First light, sir?" queried Oakes, his voice scarce above a squeak.

"I would send you immediately if it were not impracticable," stated the duke. "Nonetheless, you will leave at dawn. You will go to Dieppe and, using the *Mistress,* ferry across to Newhaven." His grace noticed Oakes quail at this suggestion, but continued. "You will then hire a coach to take you to my hunting box in Hertfordshire. Once there, I require you to choose a pointer bitch from among the most promising of the litters and bring her back to me here. I leave everything in your capable hands."

"England — dogs —" stammered a bemused Oakes, not wholly taking in the situation. "But who will dress your grace?"

"I'm sure my cousin will not begrudge me the use of his man."

"But what of your grace's boots? I mean

no offense, but Mr. Blake's valet has not the way with leather as have I."

The duke chuckled at Oakes' woebegone countenance, but nonetheless remained firm in his desire to send the valet to England. "To be left at that worthy lackey's mercy is a necessary evil, I'm afraid," he said. "I am convinced my leathers will survive your absence without any permanent damage."

With no expression on his drained countenance, Oakes drew himself erect. "If that is what your grace wishes."

"It is what I wish."

"Then I will prepare immediately, sir," and on that submissive note Oakes repaired to his own room, consoling himself with the thought that this service could do naught but enhance his employer's opinion of him.

Chapter Six

Julie had indeed cried herself into a headache, which still lingered the following morning, shortening her temper and making her feel ill. She decided to remain abed, but as a feeling of restlessness would not leave her, she drew on a wrapper of ivory silk and paced uneasily about the room. Had she but known it, the cause of her agitation had just gone down to his breakfast, but as she was unaware of this, she ordered chocolate and toast to be brought to her room. She had just sat down to this light repast when Sally entered, almost staggering under the weight of a large wax doll.

"Me come to see you," she announced, wriggling onto the sofa beside her sister. "I've called my dolly Julie, 'cause she looks like you."

Not knowing whether to take this as a compliment, Julie allowed her sister to deposit the unyielding form of the doll onto her lap. "Nurse her," demanded Sally, covering the doll with a fold of Julie's wrapper.

Cradling the doll in one arm and drawing her sister into the other, Julie voiced a question uppermost in her mind. "Do you like the duke, Sally?"

As the child gave her a puzzled look, she explained. "The gentleman whose knee you sat on and whom you kissed on Christmas Day?"

"He's pwetty," stated Sally, nodding decisively.

"Yes, I know, dear, but do you like him?"

Once more Sally vigorously nodded her head. "I like him better than Bertwam even, 'cause he called me a lady. Bertwam says I'm a baby and I'm not, am I?"

"No, love, of course not. Did the duke say anything more to you?"

"Lots, but the nasty man came to play and I didn't want him to."

"But Mr. Blake is very nice."

"Not as nice as pwetty gentlepum!"

"No, not as nice as pretty gentleman," agreed Julie pensively, a slight crease marring her brow, "and he is to leave us today."

At that moment Lady Markham entered her daughter's apartment and after a brief greeting bade her dress and join her in the hall, saying, "Our guests will be leaving in about half an hour, my dear, and it would look so well if you were to be present at their leave-taking."

"Do all our guests go today, Mama?" asked Julie casually.

"All but Mr. Blake and his cousin, my love. Did your papa not tell you that he has invited them to stay for the hunting?" There was something in her daughter's face that arrested her, and she said with some concern, "Do you feel quite well, my dear? Your countenance is slightly flushed, as if you might have a fever."

"I have no fever, Mama," replied Julie, hastily averting her face to look through the window so that her ladyship could not see the sudden gleam her words had brought to her daughter's eyes.

Still not convinced, Lady Markham cast her daughter one final look, but, as nothing further seemed amiss, she merely said, "Be a good girl and make haste. We must not seem to be lacking in manners where our guests are concerned."

At this, Lady Markham took her leave, and Julie made all haste to dress, but for as much as time was short, it did not prevent her from carefully choosing a gown of primrose taffeta that she knew became her well, or from directing her maid to take special care over the dressing of her hair.

The duke, however, was quite ignorant of these preparations in his honor.

Instead, he was joined by Stefan in the games room, languidly pursuing a game of billiards, while their hosts were attending the leave-takings.

"I say, Marcel, I do wish you would pay attention," complained Stefan, watching the duke absently gaze out the window.

"My apologies, coz," replied his grace, bowing slightly. "I seem forever to be offending you of late. However, it is not my intention. See, you now have my full attention." Looking at the table, he saw that all the balls had been cleared, and he said with a rueful grin, "So, I am beaten already! I must indeed be entering my dotage to have let you win so easily."

Impatiently snapping his cue back into the rack, Stefan complained, "Perhaps if you had looked to what you were doing in the first place I would not have won at all. Just what is the matter with you, Marcel? You seem to be in one of your toplofty moods today. Has someone displeased you?"

"Nothing of the kind," replied the duke, also replacing his cue, "but if truth be told, I'm beginning to wish myself back in Paris."

"But yesterday you agreed —"

"That's as may be, but pon rep, if I hadn't arranged for Oakes to return here, I would leave today along with the other guests. But as it is, I must await his return."

"You dumbfound me, Marcel. I cannot understand your motives. Just what the devil did you send him chasing back to England for in the first place?"

"As I explained, Stefan, a whim, a mere whim."

"You know, Marcel, you must think me pretty dim," said Stefan, trying hard to read his cousin's inscrutable countenance. "First of all, you try to fadge me off with a story about walking into doors, and now you start having sudden whims that cause your valet to go posthaste to England. I'm not that hen-witted, you know."

His grace lifted a sardonic brow. "Your powers of perception never cease to amaze me," he said with a mocking smile. "However, I am in no mood to gratify your inquisitive nature, and I advise you to let the subject drop!"

"Damn, but you're a cold fish," muttered Stefan with disapproval, but he dared say no more on the subject and instead suggested a walk in Sefron's grounds.

■ ■ ■ ■

The cousins stepped out onto the paved walk leading to the orchard, and with one oblivious to the chill wind against which his satin coat was no proof, and the other deeming it better not to complain, they slowly wended their way along a laurel walk.

"If you really desire to return to Paris, Marcel, we could always tell his lordship that you have remembered some urgent business and must return immediately," mused Stefan as he paced beside his cousin. "That is, of course, if you really want to leave Sefron. But why the sudden change of mind?"

Marcel would not explain his motives. How could he, when they were not entirely clear to himself? All he knew was that he was in danger of succumbing to emotions to which he had thought himself impervious. To take Stefan into his confidence would make him seem like a fool. He had reasoned that if he could distance himself from the cause of his emotional unrest, sense would once more return, but the thought of leaving proved too unwelcome, and he said, "I'm afraid courtesy binds us, and we must stay, but as soon as Oakes returns, we shall depart."

"But why?"

"My dear Stefan, you know me, a mere —"

"Don't tell me. I can guess. A whim, a mere whim. Am I correct?"

"Precisely so, dear cousin. A whim, nothing more."

"Of late you have become the most whimsical of fellows, Marcel. It's a wonder you're not deranged. One is in danger of wondering at your motives."

"Have no fear, coz. Even though at times I do not display the fact, I am still in full possession of my faculties. Ah, but do I perceive Master Bertram approaching? He seems determined that we should not avoid him."

Bertram, a tall dark youth of twenty-one, met up with the cousins as they were about to turn into the orchard, and after a polite greeting he addressed the duke. "Sir, I would not wish to put myself forward in any way, but I have heard that you are an excellent judge of horseflesh. I was wondering, therefore, if you would come to the stables and look over a stallion I have just purchased. He's got the devil's own temper, but with such conformation that, even against my father's wishes, I couldn't resist buying him."

The duke smiled kindly at Bertram, who seemed to stand slightly in awe of him. "If you will but lead the way, I will follow," he said, thinking that this could be the diversion he needed.

"But you are not dressed for the stables," insisted Stefan in urgent undertones, "and you know how difficult it is to remove the odor of horses from one's raiments!"

His grace favored him with one of his most disdainful glances. "You are not compelled to accompany us," he said. "You can always return to the house."

Stefan had no mind to return to Sefron and instead grudgingly kept step with the duke and Bertram. As the trio entered the stable yard, the sound of tearing wood assailed their ears as a frightened groom ran out of a loose box.

"What's wrong, Leon?" asked Bertram, starting forward at a run. "That's the new horse's box, isn't it?"

"*Oui, monsieur,* and never again will I enter it," said the groom vehemently. "That 'orse is named right. *Satanas.*"

"What the devil's going on?" asked Bertram, going to the door of the loose box and gazing into its dim depths.

"The 'orse will not stand still while I

groom him, and when I go to tie 'im up, 'e tears at the wood, and . . . poof, it is in splinters, and then 'e chases me. I will not go in again, monsieur. Not for a thousand louis!"

Suddenly, the horse ran wildly at the stable door, causing Bertram to hastily retreat out of its reach. It was a rich blood-chestnut, and as it stood with the whites of its eyes showing and nostrils distended to show a fiery red, it did indeed look a demon.

"Get a twitch on him," commanded Bertram, eyeing the animal warily. "I want him tied up short."

Unwilling to see such a beautiful animal restrained by a twitch, the duke laid a hand on Bertram's arm, saying, "I do not wish to interfere with your methods, but if one of your men would put a head collar on him and lead him into the yard, I would like to take a look at him."

Reluctantly, Bertram gave the order, and the groom, even though no thousand louis were forthcoming, at one look from the duke took a leather head collar off its hook by the door and entered the box. Much snorting and shuffling then ensued, but eventually he led the stallion into the yard, and it stood with legs rigid, as if ready for instant flight. A tremor ran through its whole body as it eyed the company askance; it was evident that the animal's fiery temperament was based on fear.

His grace ran a reassuring hand down the horse's satin-smooth neck, now darkened by sweat, and then by gentle degrees examined its back and legs. Satanas never moved but stood with his muscles steeled to meet the beating that must surely come. He was a huge six-year-old, and in his short six years (for three of which he had been sadly neglected and allowed to run wild, and a further three in which he had passed from owner to owner, experiencing the cruel hand of man), he had come to expect a thrashing for what had started out to be high spirits and had now turned to vice. No hand was raised against him, however, and he instead found himself being gently handled.

"If you have no objections, I would like to try him out," said his grace, turning to Bertram.

"Dash it all, coz, you can't ride him," expostulated Stefan.

"And why not?" asked his grace with raised brows.

"He will kill you."

"He may try, but I don't think he will," said Marcel, patting the horse's neck affectionately. At the sudden movement of the duke's hand, Satanas snorted and rolled his white-rimmed eyes.

"No, no, Marcel, I can't allow it," interpolated Stefan, showing no small amount of concern for the duke's safety.

"Go to the devil," replied his grace good-humoredly, in no way appreciating his cousin's concern. "You're like an old woman, Stefan. If he has me off, I will just have to get back on again. In the unlikely event that he should kill me, then my will is made out in your favor. Either way, you cannot lose."

"You are incorrigible," announced Stefan, "and a damn fool in the bargain. I'll have nothing further to do with you."

"I am greatly relieved," replied his grace, with a mocking bow. Turning to Bertram, he again repeated his request. "May I ride the horse?"

"If you wish, sir," he replied doubtfully, "but —"

"Then have him tacked up. I will be back directly." Striding back to Sefron, his grace repaired to his apartment to change into clothes more suitable for riding.

Returning to the stable yard some twenty minutes later, he could readily perceive the disapproval on Stefan's face and a look of frightened apprehension on Bertram's. It had just occurred to this worthy individual that his father might not approve of the projected ride. Having been forbidden to even attempt to mount the horse, he wondered at the prudence of allowing one of his father's guests to make the attempt.

The duke's enthusiasm for the ride had in no way abated, however, and he hoped that the physical activity might divert his thoughts from their wayward course. Satanas' beauty once more struck him most forcibly, and he ordered that he be led to the paddock.

"Marcel . . . ," began Stefan in some consternation, starting forward to stand between his cousin and the horse.

"Yes?" inquired the duke, with a sardonic lift of his brow.

"Oh, nothing. I've said all I can, only *take care.*"

"But of course," said the duke, with such mocking assurance that Stefan longed to box his ears.

Satanas, with ears nervously pricked, allowed himself to be led to the paddock and stood tensely awaiting his rider. Leaving Stefan and Bertram leaning on the paddock gate, the duke took charge of his deceptively quiet mount and, turning the stirrup, he mounted, lowering himself gently into the saddle. After asserting that the girths were secure, he gave Satanas the office to walk on. Stiff with pent-up energy, the horse moved into an uneven pace without, to the spectators' great relief, rebelling against the aids. The pressure of the duke's thighs was slight but not to be ignored and, consequently, the stallion began gradually to lengthen his stride and change into a more even gait.

His grace rode the horse to the farther end of the paddock, feeling the animal's powerful muscles ripple beneath him. He could not but appreciate that he was astride a volcano that sooner or later was bound to erupt. Even now, he could feel the first tremors of conflict begin, but while they were almost out of sight of the spectators, he cared not what happened. This was the horse for him!

A well-booted heel came into light contact with Satanas' sides, and the pressure on the reins was gently released so that the horse shot forward into a gallop. Covering the remainder of the paddock in a few strides, he took the fence that led into the adjoining pasture with an effortless ease. Realizing that the slightest touch on the bit would

107

bring instant rebellion from the stallion, the duke gave him his head and, leaning well over the horse's withers, gently guided him with his knees.

Oblivious to both distance and obstacles alike, horse and rider gave caution to the wind, and with a demonlike enjoyment the duke saw trees pass as lightning, with no thought to care. It was as if he were intoxicated. The contours of the countryside seemed to merge into one, until a sudden rise in the ground caused the duke to check Satanas' speed, but to no avail, as the horse continued to gallop laboriously up the steep hill. The duke, deeming it time his mount was brought under control, turned him sharply to the left, attempting to draw rein, but Satanas, showing a strong will, tried to turn a full circle. Fortunately, the duke was used to the vagaries of young horses and prevented him from completing the circle, driving him back down the hill. Sweat darkened Satanas' neck and great deep chest, but his pace did not slacken. Once more achieving level ground, the duke allowed him his head. Both horse and rider, exhilarated by the turn of speed, became as one, the duke being but a further extension of the steely muscle and nerve of the horse. A large hedge loomed ominously ahead, but without even the slightest check in speed, the duo cleared it easily. The duke's whole concentration was centered on the horse, and he scarcely noticed the terrain they covered.

Eventually, Satanas' sides began to heave, and the duke began to steady his hitherto breakneck speed, calming the horse with his voice. A passion for possession gripped him. Satanas must be his.

Caressing the stallion's neck and feeling the firm flesh damp beneath his palm, he gave a short laugh at the thought of Stefan and Bertram awaiting him at the stables, probably confirmed in their belief that he had by now broken his neck.

The ride had done much to dispel his pensive mood of the morning. Satanas was now content to obey his commands, and a decided rapport existed between horse and rider. It was not strange, therefore, that as he wended his way back to Sefron, his thoughts should return to Julie. This *tender* was new to him; not even as a callow youth had his affections been so readily engaged, and it puzzled him slightly that on so short an acquaintance he could become so firmly attached. The hasty resolve to quit Sefron had been dismissed, the notion proving more unwelcome than he cared to admit.

But then, he thought with a sigh, *I have had passing fancies before, and they have proved to be no more lasting than the first. Therefore, my affections are not to be trusted.*

As he approached the paddock he perceived his cousin pacing the cobbles of the stable yard in a most agitated fashion. "It seems we have caused some concern," he chuckled, once more caressing Satanas' fine neck. "Come, it is time we made amends," and as one they cleared the fence and cantered across the paddock.

At sight of the duke, Stefan ran quickly to open the gate. Favoring his cousin with a dark scowl, he demanded, "Where the devil have you been? You've been gone this hour and more. Lord Markham has torn poor Bertram off a strip and sent him in search of you."

"Your concern does you credit," said Marcel, amused by the intensity of Stefan's unease on his behalf. Lightly dismounting, he led Satanas into the stable yard. "I'm sorry Bertram has been gudgeoned for my sake. Did you not tell his lordship it was my own doing?"

"Devil a bit, but he blames the boy. Says he should never have bought the horse in the first place and told him to get rid of it."

110

"Then I will be more than willing to take it off his hands," averred the duke, peeling off his riding gloves. "In fact, that was my very intention. By-the-bye, should we not send someone out to fetch the young jack-a-napes back before he scours the country-side looking for a corpse that doesn't exist?"

Stefan grinned reluctantly. "Knew it would take more than a horse to kill you," he said. "Told 'em so, but they wouldn't believe me. Never seen such a lot of hen-worriers in all my life!"

"I appreciate your confidence in me," replied his grace sardonically. Then, seeing the groom standing open-mouthed, as if beholding an apparition, he commanded, "Take Satanas and walk him until he has cooled," handing the horse over to the astonished man. "When he is quite cool, you may allow him to drink, but not before." Noting the amazement on the groom's face, the duke demanded, "What ails you now?"

"*Monseigneur* is all right?" the groom asked, as if disbelieving his eyes.

"As you see, I returned unscathed," replied the duke, thoroughly weary of the subject. "Send someone in search of your young master. It would not do to have him careering over the countryside. Tell him all is well."

"Oui," replied the groom in revered tones. "This very minute, *monseigneur.*"

The cousins set to return to Sefron, but Stefan, about to link arms with the duke, hastily withdrew his arm and took to the other side of the path. The duke fixed him with a quizzing gaze and asked with some surprise, "What's to do now?"

"Shall we say the aroma of the stables?" replied Stefan raising his handkerchief delicately to his nostrils in mock horror. "Your ride has not exactly enhanced your desirability, Marcel."

"Nodcock!" replied his grace good-humoredly, and strode off to his room to change.

CHAPTER SEVEN

Once more resplendent — in a coat of amber velvet, satin knee breeches, and a waistcoat of dull gold — the duke added the final touch of a diamond pin in his frothing cravat of Melchin lace. He surveyed the results of his hour-long labors with some trepidation. It would indeed seem an age to Oakes' return, for while the duke did not like to admit it, his valet did have a certain way with a neck-cloth that was quite his own, and, while his grace did not aspire to being a tulip of fashion, it was generally agreed among his cronies that he was a top-rigger. It was still some two hours to supper, and the duke, finding that when he was left alone his thoughts took a fanciful turn, decided to seek diversion from the contents of the library. It had been quite some while since he had found the time or the inclination to read, but if his thoughts were to be channeled in a different direction, he needed something other than a certain pair of twinkling blue eyes to fill them. Leaving his room, he found his way down to the library.

Unfortunately, the duke's intention of reading was forestalled, for no sooner had he entered the room than he found that Lord Markham had had the self-same idea. His lordship sat ensconced in a large, winged, fireside chair, avidly perusing the daily journals he had dispatched from London each week.

"Come in, come in," he hailed as the duke, hoping himself to be unobserved, prepared to make good his retreat. "Glad to see you in one piece, lad. What a turn you gave us all, no thanks to that graceless son of mine and his wretched horse. Your cousin said that you were a bruising good rider, but one can never tell in these matters. Wouldn't do to have a guest break his neck."

"You must forgive me," drawled the duke at his most haughty. "It was not my intention to disturb you."

"Nonsense, nonsense," Lord Markham said and smiled, impervious to the duke's cool manner and indicating a chair at the opposite side of the hearth. "Here, take a seat and join me in a glass of canary, and by-the-bye, I think we have stood on ceremony long enough. You know my name is

Jonathan as well as I know yours is Marcel."

"Just so — Jonathan," replied his grace languidly, as his lordship handed him a glass of wine.

"You're a cool one, make no mistake," chuckled his lordship, seating himself opposite the duke, "but I warn you, Marcel, sooner or later you will have to get off that high horse of yours. Not that I don't admire you for it — fact is, I do — but damn, you have to be human sometimes, my boy. Proved that you can be too. Saw you with my youngest daughter only the other day. Quite taken with you, she was."

His grace smiled ruefully at his companion; he *was* slightly human, after all. "I must be coming to a sad pass when two people, in the space of a day, reproach me for my toplofty manners. Stefan took me to task only this morning. No, no," he said, grinning contritely as he raised his hand to silence Lord Markham, who was about to beg his forgiveness for such a forthright speech. "Fact is, Stefan thinks me a proper cold fish. I only hope I can prove you both wrong."

Just at that moment a light scratching on the door interrupted their discourse. "Enter," called his lordship, pouring himself and his guest yet another glass of canary.

115

Julie stood in the doorway, looking slightly confused. "Your pardon, Papa. I thought you alone. I came only to tell you that supper is put back half an hour to enable Bertram to be present, as he still needs to change."

"Young dolt!" expostulated his lordship, giving full vent to his opinion of his eldest son. Extending his hand, he beckoned his daughter into the room. "Won't you join us, my dear? I'm sure Marcel will have no objections."

Smiling, the duke rose to offer his seat, and, dropping a slight curtsy, Julie occupied the chair he proffered, the duke then taking the chesterfield slightly to the left of his companions.

Lord Markham, though not usually a very observant parent, could not help but perceive the slight flush on his daughter's cheek and the smile in her eyes as they alighted upon the duke, and, although it took him quite by surprise, he did not wholly dislike it. Indeed, he would not be too displeased if there were signs of a match here, for he liked the duke well enough and he wished to have his daughter creditably settled. He was jumping the gun and he knew it. Women were such unpredictable creatures and men — well, they had their fancies, as who knew better than he, and at the duke's age they rarely lasted above a sennight. It was then with equal surprise that he saw the duke's mien soften and a slight smile curve his stern lips. Then the moment was gone, and the same satirical look had crossed his visage, and his lordship wondered if he had imagined the whole, for now there was no trace of softness in the hard, handsome face before him.

For a moment, but only a moment, the duke had allowed himself to study the charming profile proffered before him as Julie related some amusing domestic detail to her father, but then, on a sudden resolve, he rose to go. "You will excuse me — er — Jonathan," he drawled, adjusting the foaming lace at his wrists. "I recollect a letter that must be written. I will intrude on your peace no longer."

Lord Markham, casting a quizzical look upon him, could not resist an inward smile. It would take some time to understand this duke, who was so high in the instep, Markham thought, but he could already perceive a crack in the duke's hitherto iron defense. "I would not wish to keep you," he beamed, and it was with some chagrin that the duke noted the genuine amusement in his host's voice.

Marcel was not destined for a dignified retreat, however. He had no sooner taken a step toward the door than it was flung open and a small fury deposited herself against his legs, sending him reeling back to the chesterfield. Sally, uttering screams of delight at having found him, thrust her doll, now clad only in the flimsiest chemise, onto the duke's lap and demanded, "Pretty gentlepum nurse her."

The look of abject amazement that flitted across the duke's countenance was just too much for Lord Markham and his daughter, who joined together in unrestrained mirth. Perceiving what a figure of fun he must have cut, his grace gave a shout of laughter and added his tones to those of his companions, while Sally paraded up and down the hearth, well aware that she had been the cause of such hilarity.

Julie was the first to recover some semblance of composure, and in a voice still shaking with laughter tried to control her jubilant sister. The duke, however, frustrated all her efforts by reaching out and catching Sally under the arms. Tossing her high into the air, he finally sat her on his knee.

"You young temptress," he said and laughed. "Faith, but you are the first young lady to knock me so completely off my feet."

Eyeing the doll with some misgiving, he gingerly raised her by the arm, saying, in mock solemnity, "I must ask you to remove this other — er — lady from my lap. Alas, she is not suitably attired to appear in public!"

Sally kneeled on the duke's lap and, clasping her strong little arms about his neck, hugged him so hard that he gave up any hope of his lace cravat ever being of use again. Lord Markham, however, came to his rescue by taking his young daughter into his arms.

"You imp," he said with a chuckle. "Have you no shame? If you were but a few years older, you would be termed a hussy. All this excitement is not good for you. Whatever your mama would say, I shudder to think. Now, take your doll and go back to the nursery."

"No," she said defiantly, trying to wriggle free of her father's arms. "I want pretty gentlepum."

"For heaven's sake, don't call me that," pleaded the duke, halfway between amusement and genuine embarrassment.

"You should say 'your grace,'" corrected Julie.

"Not a bit of it," laughed the duke. "She shall call me Marcel."

"Marcewl," Sally said, and chuckled triumphantly over her father's shoulder.

"That's right," approved the duke with great fortitude, wincing only slightly at hearing his name so lacerated. Seizing the opportunity, he turned to Julie and, in a voice that had lost all amusement, asked, "Would I be asking too much for you to call me Marcel, for after all 'tis my name, and it sounds far better than 'your grace'?"

Meeting his gaze steadily, she repeated, "Marcel," and he noticed how readily it sprang to her lips.

Sally had taken possession of her doll once more, and Lord Markham, setting her on her feet, faced her in the direction of the door and commanded, "Nursery." He gave her a gentle push to help her on her way, but now the small whirlwind of a moment before had become a tired little girl as she made her way toward the door, dragging her doll, which now seemed far too large for her tiny arms, behind her. She looked such a dejected little being that his grace took pity on her and, striding forward, lifted her gently into his arms. Dropping her doll, she snuggled happily against him.

"What a child!" chuckled his lordship. "It would seem she has made a conquest.

Already she knows the way to a man's heart."

His grace gave a smile that was difficult to define and, turning, made his way into the hall, intent on returning his young tormentor to the nursery, for she was already half asleep. Picking up the doll, Julie made to follow him, but her father stayed her for a moment. "He's learning," he said softly. "Duke or no duke, he's learning."

That evening, supper was even livelier than usual. Stefan was discussing the various points of hunting with his lordship, Bertram was extolling the beauty of Satanas with the duke while reluctantly arranging his sale, and Julie and Charlotte discussed what to wear at the New Year's Eve ball. Lady Markham presided over the whole, well contented with the success of the evening. She had recently returned from the nursery, where the younger members of the family dined, and was feeling very proud of her offspring, all of whom were well and in fine spirits. Conversation flowed as easily as wine, and, with the astuteness of a mother, she noticed the ready blush that mounted her daughter's cheek whenever his grace addressed her. *'Tis well,* she thought. *'Tis well.*

She liked this duke, despite his distant manner.

When supper was finally over, the gentlemen did not linger over their port as was their usual wont but instead joined the ladies in the drawing room. Charlotte strummed idly on the harpsichord while Lady Markham sat by the fire completing her intricate embroidery.

Upon entering the room, his grace had glanced around for Julie, and a slight frown creased his brow as she was not immediately visible. As his gaze penetrated the shadows of a windowed alcove, however, he perceived her gazing through the frosted casement at the almost too brilliant moon and flickering stars.

Everyone ranged around the fire, but his grace, as if magnetically drawn, left the group and, crossing the room, stood quietly behind Julie. "Lady moon, lady moon, where are you roaming?" he quoted softly.

Julie turned, slightly startled, for she had not been aware of his presence, but then her gaze softened into a welcome, and she did not object as he took a seat beside her, the heavy curtain almost obscuring them from view. "She is beautiful, our moon, is she not?" she asked, once more returning her gaze to the window.

The duke did not reply, for it was not the moon that he was admiring but the sweet oval of his companion's face as the moon cast it from the shadows with its silvery light. This would not do, however — it was too dangerous to think along these lines. So, instead, he rallied his forces of concentration.

"Tell me what you thought of London while you were there," he said, as Julie finally turned toward him.

For a moment, she studied the folds of her skirts and then, looking up, said, " 'Tis a beautiful city, but one can feel so alone within its walls."

"Were you lonely, *chéri?*" he asked softly.

"Sometimes," she replied pensively. "When my aunt was ill, I was left very much to my own devices, and at times I longed for company other than my cousin John."

"He bored you?" queried his grace, not without some interest.

"No, no, of course not, but he would insist on pressing his suit, even though I emphatically rejected him."

"He offered for you?" asked the duke, more sharply than he intended.

"And why not?"

"Why not indeed?" he mused. "But why did you find his suit so unfavorable?"

123

"He would be kind, I suppose," she said thoughtfully,

"Kind," he expostulated. "Kindness is all you ask of a husband?"

"But you did not let me finish, sir. What I wished to say is that he would be kind, but I did not love him, and therefore it was useless for him to continue pressuring me to accept."

For a moment the duke was silent, gazing thoughtfully at the moon and marveling at its nearness. "Do you believe in love?" he asked in deceptively light tones, not trusting himself to face his companion.

"Yes, I believe in love," she answered softly. Now it was Julie's turn to study the handsome profile set before her, and for that moment she knew an impulse to try to smooth the slight frown that troubled his brow. "Although it is *la mode* for a *marriage du convenience* to be arranged between families, my parents married for love, and if I should marry, it will be for the same reason."

"Ah, then you returned from London with a whole heart?" he asked with more than idle curiosity.

"Not entirely," she replied, mischievously peeping up at him through lowered lashes.

"To whom was it lost, if not your cousin?"

he demanded with more asperity than he had intended as he swung around to face her.

With an infectious chuckle she replied, "I bought the finest gray mare you ever did see, and it fair broke my heart to leave her behind. Does that satisfy your grace?"

"Ah, my true desserts," he said, smiling in mock penitence. "I am well served, but, as I remember, you were to call me Marcel."

Dimpling, she teased lightly, "It does not suit you."

"And pray why not, for 'tis my name?"

"I have called you 'your grace' for too long."

"Let it be Marcel or nothing," he replied with what dignity he could muster.

"Very well, I suppose I must call you Marcel, if only to pacify you," she said, smiling warmly and coloring rosily as the duke briefly caught her hand in his.

Although they were in the shadows of the alcove, their movements had not gone unnoticed by her ladyship, who had kept a north eye on her daughter while appearing engrossed in her stitchery. Seeing the expression on the duke's face, although it gratified her heart, made her decide that now was the time to interrupt their intimate *tête-à-tête.* "Will you favor us with a song, my love?" she called to her eldest daughter and noted with what reluctance Julie left the duke's side, for she would have been content to spend the evening there.

Julie's voice was not strong, but the tones were sweet, and the French lullabies she sang suited her perfectly. The evening seemed to fly by. Further discourse with the duke was not possible, and it was not long before each one in turn forsook the warmth of the hearth for the comforts of bed.

The duke, however, did not immediately seek repose. Instead, he donned his elegant banyan and, sitting by the fire in his apartment, idly flicked through the sporting papers procured from the library for him by an impassive lackey. Unsurprisingly, however, he found his attention was wont to wander, and he was therefore just preparing to retire when there was a knock on his door. With a groan and a great show of reluctance (for he had guessed the only one who would be calling at so late an hour), he once more slipped his banyan over his shoulders and called *"Entrée"* in a weary voice.

As expected, Stefan stepped over the threshold and, carefully closing the heavy door behind him, with a rather sheepish grin bade his cousin *bon soir.*

126

"I am sure that it is not to wish me good evening that you keep me from my bed," snapped the duke, not in the best of humors.

"No, coz, I assure you," said Stefan. "It's just that I've been thinking —"

"A fact that amazes me," mocked the duke, taking in the slightly swaying figure before him. "And what, may I ask, have you been thinking about? Though why it should be of interest to me, I have no notion."

"Well, coz, when we were in Paris I said you were going soft. I'm sorry, Marcel, I was wrong. Never been more up to the nines in your life, a real prime-un. No one could hoodwink you."

"Have you been drinking?" asked his grace suspiciously, his eyes narrowing as Stefan slowly lowered himself into a chair.

"Just a quick one, or two, with Lord M, don't you know," he admitted ruefully, "but I needed it to come and apologize to you for what I said. Unforgivable, I know, and it's been plaguing me these four days or more. When I found out how you came by that deuced ugly bruise on your face, well, I just had to apologize."

His grace almost pounced upon Stefan. "You know how I got the bruise," he said tightly through clenched teeth, and then, incredulously, "Julie hasn't told you . . ."

"No, no, rest assured, not a word has passed her lips. It was the gardener! He saw everything through the window and told me all about it when I was waiting for you at the stables this morning."

"Nom de Dieu," groaned the duke, turning away. "The whole household will know by morning."

"Not from me," assured Stefan, "and I've told the gardener what will happen if he so much as utters a word."

"Many thanks," breathed the duke, forcing a smile. "I know I can count on you." Then on a lighter note, he added, "At least your curiosity is sated, and now you won't think me fool enough to have walked into a door."

"Never did," replied Stefan rather thickly. "Always thought it was a mill. Said so at the time, if you remember, but from what I hear, you showed to great advantage, a prime turn-up, I should imagine. Wish I'd been there!"

"Thankfully, you were not," said the duke with a grin. "Now away with you if you wish to see sleep this side of midnight." Then, with a complete change of mood: "By-the-bye, I have a mind to join you at the hunt tomorrow. I never know my luck. Coustellet may decide to grace us with his presence, and, if you remember, we have a score to settle."

Stefan rose somewhat unsteadily. "Do you think it wise, Marcel? Better to let sleeping dogs lie, don't you think? You thrashed the man once. Don't say you have to do it again. Think of Julie. Don't want a breath of scandal. Not the thing, you know."

"Oh, go to bed," said the duke with some exasperation. "Trust me, Stefan. I'm not a Banbury-babe."

"No, slap up to the nines," he agreed, "but just take care. I have an affection for you, coz. Don't wish to see you done up. Now I will wish you *bonne nuit,* for I find myself exceedingly weary."

"Good night," returned the duke as Stefan made his somewhat rocking departure, and he repaired to his bed, snuffing the candle and lying back on the large lace pillows. Repose was not so easily won, however, and it was almost two hours before his grace slipped into its hitherto elusive depths.

CHAPTER EIGHT

The duke shuddered involuntarily as he surveyed what could be seen of the garden from his bedroom window. Droplets made by the mist hung from tree and grass alike, while clouds of swirling fog impaired visibility. *Hardly the day for a hunt,* he thought, but it was not the proposed sport that held the attraction, at least not on this particular morning. He had a meaner quarry in view. As yet, he had formed no firm plan of action, but he assured himself that he would make full use of whatever opportunity might present itself.

The gentlemen of the household had breakfasted early, making of it a hearty meal of beef and ale, for who would know if they would partake of a luncheon if sport was good? Bertram had been particularly pleased that the duke was to join them, confiding in his father that he thought his grace a bruising good rider and a top-sawyer and that Bertram was by now firm in his opinion that the duke was a first-rate fellow. The duke, however, was oblivious to the idolatry he inspired in this young man's breast and, while taking a liking to Bertram for his own sake, made mental note to steer clear of his company during the hunt, as this would not suit his purpose.

Coustellet had succeeded where others had failed by arousing in him a cold anger and a deadly determination for reprisal. Until he had come to Sefron, the duke had not believed himself susceptible to such a variety of emotions. Confident in his own ability, he had formerly treated affairs of honor with a bored indifference. On this occasion, however, it was not on his own account that he sought retribution, making his desire all the more deadly.

It was no mean feat to shrug himself into his well-fitting riding coat of olive leather without the assistance of Oakes. Although temporarily without this worthy's service, his top boots, despite being prepared by Stefan's valet, had not suffered in the slightest, and his cream buckskin breeches and waistcoat were without a crease. All this, however, went unnoticed as he buckled a rapier of the finest steel about his hips. Hiding the intricate workings of the hilt beneath the folds of his coat, he hoped it would not draw notice, as swords were not usually worn to the hunt, and his motives might be suspect. Finally adjusting the snowlike stock that surrounded his throat, he surveyed the whole effect in a gilt-edged mirror placed over the mantel. While not thoroughly satisfied with his image, he decided that he would do and, collecting his gloves and whip, prepared to join the others.

There were to be no ladies present at this morning's hunt, or so Lord Markham had informed him over breakfast. "More a man's sport, anyway," Markham had confided. "Petticoats are best out of the way, especially on a day like this. Should imagine a field of about thirty will show — that is, if this damn mist don't keep 'em away. Most of me neighbors are strong followers, so I don't suppose a bit of weather will deter 'em!" It was on this that the duke was relying, as Coustellet's estates lay only three miles or so south of Sefron's boundaries.

His grace reached the large hall just as the grooms brought the horses to stand before the shallow stone steps leading to Sefron's frontage, the mount's hooves sounding impatient on the loose gravel of the driveway. Stefan stood resting his shoulders against the doorjamb with his hands thrust deep into his breeches pockets. The tricorn he wore at a slight angle shadowed a countenance somewhat the worse for wear after his excesses of the previous night. He had toyed with breakfast, resisted the "hair of the dog" and was at this moment fervently hoping that his lordship would abandon the hunt in favor of a less energetic occupation.

Sauntering to stand beside his cousin, the duke noted with some disgust Stefan's obviously delicate condition. "I trust you slept well," he scorned, "or could that be the reason why you are not as yet up-to-the-nines?"

"Go to blazes, Marcel," snapped Stefan, pressing a shaking hand to his brow. "You know full well why I'm not as yet in top rig."

"My dear cousin, my concern was solely for your health, but as I can see you are in no mood for company, I will relieve you of mine until your mood takes a complete turnabout. I would appreciate it, however, if you would refrain from tipping the full on the eve of a hunt, if only for your own safety."

"Devil take you, Marcel," snarled Stefan, starting forward toward the steps. "I'm out of me cradle, don't you know," and with this he flung sullenly down the steps to painfully mount his horse, visibly wincing at the exertion.

The damp seemed to strike through the duke's coat. Visibility was none too good. He wondered at the sense of hunting on such a day as this, but it did not seem to worry Lord Markham, who was urging everyone to mount as quickly as possible. Other riders were now joining those from Sefron, but it was in vain that the duke searched their ranks for Coustellet, and his grace knew a moment's irritation. Warming porter was being offered as a stirrup cup by the lackeys carrying large silver trays. His grace was mounted on a well-set-up gray mare of about sixteen hands high. "Heart like a lion," his lordship had informed him. "A real sweet goer." The duke drew on his deerskin gauntlets, the reins already damp with the mist, and checked the mare's impulse to move off as the handlers brought the hounds from the kennels. The dogs ran eagerly among the horses until they were called to heel by the whip, and then they were all eagerness to be away. They, at least, were not affected by the depressing weather. Tongues lolling and tails wagging, they set out in the wake of their master, content at the moment to follow obediently.

The members of the hunt, a somewhat

diminished number from that which Lord Markham had predicted, made their way down Sefron's sweeping drive and out into the narrow lane. His grace, deeming it best to keep to the rear, kept Stefan just in sight some ten yards in front of him, but as they forsook the lane in favor of an open field, Stefan fell farther behind, the duke overtaking him as they cantered over the sodden ground. It seemed that the hunt was not to be as fruitful as the duke had hoped, the fog only adding to his annoyance by becoming thicker.

Suddenly, Marcel was aware of someone riding alongside him. It was Stefan. Gone were the signs of his previous disorders, and it was now a worried frown that creased his brow. "Did you see who joined us as we turned in off the lane?" he asked, bringing his horse in even closer to the duke's side. The mist made of his words just muffled sounds, but grasping his meaning, the duke swung full in the saddle to see Coustellet keeping well to the farther side of the hunt. He had also seen the duke, and there was no mistaking the animosity that passed between them. A sardonic smile spread over the duke's countenance as, bending low in the saddle, he favored Coustellet with a courtly bow. This was received with no small amount of chagrin, but, managing to keep his head, Coustellet proffered a brief nod in return.

"So, now the quarry arrives," purred the duke as they drew rein beside a coppice and waited while the whip sent in the hounds. Stefan, stealing a glance at his cousin, could not suppress a slight shudder. His grace sat on the mare as one made of stone, looking neither right nor left, his eyes taking on a satanic gleam. This was the duke at his most awful, and Stefan had no mind to incur his wrath by breaking his reverie to plead sanity, for he knew the duke was at that moment beyond reasoning. Suddenly, a brace of wood pigeons, disturbed by the hounds, flew out from the trees, startling both horses and riders alike, and in that moment the duke made his move. The sardonic smile returning to his lips, he turned the mare away from the remainder of the group as they sought to bring their mounts under control and instead quietly made his way to Coustellet's side.

"A good day for a hunt," he mocked softly, obviously startling the gentleman for yet a second time. "So pleased you could find the time to join us. I can assure you, the day would have been lost without the pleasure of your company," and again he gave a most unpleasant smile.

Coustellet reddened visibly, his temper boiling, enabling him to give only a spluttered reply. "Damn you, Lear," he seethed through clenched teeth, his large cumbersome frame taut. "I, too, had hopes of a meeting. We yet have a score to settle."

"Just so, *mon ami.* Our last encounter had a far from satisfactory conclusion. I cannot but lament your lack of finesse in resorting to the use of a footstool. Effective, I can assure you, but not at all the thing. However, it is not our turn of fisticuffs that brings about this meeting, as I am sure you are aware, but your conduct toward a certain young lady. It is obvious that she finds your presence, let alone your attentions, repugnant to the extreme. I am here to ensure that you will not trouble her again."

Coustellet's countenance darkened further still. "None of your damn business," he growled.

"That, *mon cher,* is where you are quite mistaken," countered the duke smoothly. "It is very much my business. I have made it so, a fact that compels me to teach you a lesson, and on this very day, unless I am much mistaken."

Automatically Coustellet half withdrew the rapier that he now habitually wore in anticipation of meeting his adversary, and in that moment the huntsman blew the gone away, as with a flash of red a fox broke cover on the far side of the coppice. Coustellet was forced to sheath his sword; both he and the duke were carried along on the tide of horse and rider as the hunt gave chase, the duke's mare keeping but a length in front of Coustellet's mount.

Stefan, who seemingly had been the only witness to the heated exchange, tried vainly to reach the duke's side, but the press of the field kept a good distance between them, thus frustrating all his efforts. It was difficult trying to keep within sight of hounds; visibility had deteriorated, and as the field spread out Stefan knew a moment of panic as he completely lost sight of his cousin and Coustellet. By now, he could see only those immediately in front of him. The country was unfamiliar, and it took all his wits to negotiate the obstacles that seemed to loom suddenly in front of him.

The duke was faring no better. Both he and Coustellet seemed to have lost touch with the hunt altogether. Surrounded now by the swirling, oppressive grayness, they appeared to be in a world of their own. This was the opportunity the duke had been waiting for, and it would serve his purpose admirably.

Bringing his mare to a sudden halt, he swung her full to meet Coustellet, who was forced to bring his horse to a standstill. With a cold detachment, the duke observed his opponent's horse plunge wildly about and take all its rider's strength to bring it under control.

When the horse finally quieted sufficiently for Coustellet to face his tormentor, the duke gave a mocking bow. "My felicitations, friend," he scoffed. "Prettily done. The weather has served us well. We are quite alone and at liberty to continue our *tête-à-tête* unobserved. I am certain you are as eager as I to see an end to the affair. I am sure I need not remind you that should any breath of scandal attach itself to the young lady in question, it will be your life you forfeit and not just your reputation. Now, if you will do me the pleasure of dismounting . . ."

Coustellet threw himself from his saddle, fury showing in every line. In his haste, he did not wait to remove his coat but drew his rapier, flexing its thin blade between nervous hands. His grace dismounted — no further words were needed — and, removing his coat and waistcoat, withdrew his sword from its intricate scabbard. Flashing his blade in a brief salute, he bade Coustellet *en garde.*

The pause was but slight before the blades engaged, Coustellet attacking wildly in his fury, the duke parrying each thrust with a cold determination, the hilt of his sword damp with the mist. Steel scraped against steel, the hissing of the metal becoming almost hypnotic. Coustellet was not as ineffectual as his ungainly stature would suggest. His methods, although rustic, were effective, affording the duke some grim satisfaction, for he would not have welcomed an easy victory. Despite the chill, Coustellet was sweating profusely, not daring to wipe the moisture from his eyes should in that instant the duke choose to strike.

Their booted feet thudded dully on the turf as their breathing became labored. Coustellet, convinced that his lungs would burst, put all his weight behind a sudden thrust that slashed at the duke's powerful chest and, momentarily breaking through his guard, left a deep gash of some ten inches in length. The blood sluggishly seeped from the wound, staining the startling whiteness of the duke's shirt, but he checked but momentarily. For the briefest

140

instant, there had been a slight lapse in his concentration, but now, driving Coustellet back, he opened his cheek from brow to chin and noted with some satisfaction the scarlet start. Like a cat playing with a mouse, the duke now attacked, taking full advantage of the fact that his opponent was visibly tiring.

Coustellet's movements became wilder and more awkward. The pain in his arm and wrist made it more difficult to recover his stroke, and he found himself floundering in his attack. His guard became weaker, the duke seeming to loom even larger before his misted eyes.

In an instant it was over. Coustellet sank to the ground, dropping his sword to grip at the white-hot wound below his left shoulder that the duke's blade had made in one awful moment. The world revolved before him, rendering him almost senseless, the duke's voice reaching him as from a great distance.

"A much more satisfactory ending to the affair, I believe," the duke said, sheathing his sword. "I think you will find I have not dealt you a fatal blow, though for the moment it may seem so. Come, let me help you to your horse. You should seek a physician immediately."

With a great effort, Coustellet managed to

shrug away the duke's helping hand, dragging himself to his feet to stand rocking before his opponent. All life seemed to have drained away from his large body, and as the duke brought his horse to him, he begrudgingly accepted his assistance to mount. Slumping heavily over the horse's withers, he had but enough strength to turn it in the direction of his estates.

Watching him go, the duke became aware of the watery sun that now attempted to appear, and, as if having served its purpose, the mist had started to lift. It was not, however, until he came to don his discarded coat and waistcoat that he once more became aware of his own injury. The wound was stiff, and his shirtfront had become sodden. He would, it seemed, be in need of a sawbones himself, for his wound would need professional attention. It would be too dangerous at Sefron, however.

CHAPTER NINE

Sefron's large stables were a veritable hive of activity as the duke rode the mare into the cobbled square. Almost twenty mounts had been ridden to hounds that day, and it seemed not strange that he should arrive in the yard some short while after the others, his late arrival being attributed to the fog. His grace dismounted and handed the mare to a waiting groom. Only the grim line about his lips betrayed the effort it cost him, no one noticing that his coat was unfashionably fastened across his chest or the forced straightening of his shoulders as he strode from the yard.

Entering Sefron by a side door, he found it necessary to steady himself against an elegantly decorated wall for the space of a second. Bracing his hand against the wall and straightening his shoulders, he pushed himself erect. This would not do; no one must know of his injury. He decided he would have need of Stefan's services, however, and, entering the large hall, sent a lackey in search of him with the request that he should attend the duke in his apartment immediately.

Mounting the stairs, he made light use of the rosewood banister, and it was with no small amount of relief that he achieved his bedchamber without encountering anyone of the household. It would seem everyone was either changing or resting after the exertions of the hunt.

Entering his room, the duke stood for a moment with his back resting against the door. A large log fire burned welcomingly in the hearth, a vivid contrast to the chills of the day, and a winged chair had been placed invitingly close to the copper fender by some thoughtful lackey mindful of the duke's comfort. Painfully, his grace crossed the room and gratefully sank into the chair, resting his head, eyes closed, against the high back and slowly easing his long legs out in front of him toward the grate. There was by now a dull throbbing in his chest, and as the clock on the mantel chimed the quarter, he wondered what could be keeping his cousin.

After what seemed an interminable age, the door was unceremoniously flung open, admitting Stefan in some state of disarray, and seeing the duke apparently taking his ease, Stefan almost slammed the door shut. "What the devils to do now, Marcel?" he demanded, coming to the center of the room. "I've been out of my mind wondering what happened to you and Coustellet. Didn't know what to think, you with murder in your eyes galloping all over the countryside like your precious Satanas. Then just as I'm in the middle of changing, this damn lackey —" He suddenly stopped his remonstrating midsentence as, fully facing the duke, he took in his cousin's ashen face. "By all the saints, what the —" he began, but the duke forestalled him by raising a restraining hand and giving a wan smile.

"I'm afraid, coz, I find myself slightly indisposed, and I have need of your services. However, had I but known I was interrupting your *habillage* I would have awaited your pleasure."

"But what happened?" persisted Stefan, coming to the hearth. "Don't be so damned elusive. What of Coustellet?" Suddenly becoming aware of the paleness of the duke's countenance and the white line about his lips, Stefan's mood changed to one of concern, and he asked, "You all right? You look rather gray about the gills."

"Hold hard, coz. One thing at a time," replied Marcel, slipping the buttons to his coat and the now blood-darkened waistcoat to reveal the wound on his chest.

Stefan let out a silent whistle, his own visage blanching at the sight of so much blood.

"As I said, a slight indisposition, no more," said the duke, "but one that I am afraid necessitates my removal from Sefron, for no one must know of this. Coustellet once again has served me a leveler, but I can assure you, on this occasion he fares far worse than I."

"Dead?" inquired Stefan with a great show of enthusiasm.

"Fortunately not," replied the duke. "It would not do, coz. Not this time, not here, although I must admit the temptation was great."

"But what of you, Marcel? You are in need of a leech yourself. Can't go around bleeding all over the place. It's simply not done. Won't be able to keep that a secret for long. We'll have to call in a sawbones."

"I assure you, Stefan, if we can but stop the bleeding, I will do famously, but to call for a physician would be foolhardy. It would cause too much comment, and too many questions would be asked. A sword wound is not such a common occurrence as not to excite some curiosity, for 'tis obviously no hunting accident. No, I must return to Paris on some pretext or other, but you must stay here to allay any suspicions that there is anything amiss. Now for God's sake, help me to at least bind the wound."

It was with some difficulty that Stefan aided the duke to remove his coat. "Damned good waistcoat ruined," he muttered, flinging the offending garment to the floor. His bluff manner was but a blind to cover his concern for his cousin who, while of an extremely strong constitution, had lost a deal of blood and even to Stefan's inexperienced eye looked rather drawn. The duke flinched but slightly as his shirt was removed, laying bare his powerful chest, which was now caked with drying blood. Fortunately, a ewer of hot water and a china basin had been provided for the duke's refreshment after the hunt, and it was to this that Stefan now turned, using one of the towels of fine linen to clean the wound.

Bearing his cousin's ministrations with a stoicism born of necessity, the duke sat with eyes closed and hands gripping the arms of the chair. Once the wound was cleaned, Stefan made a pad from another towel with three of the duke's snowy stocks providing a makeshift bandage.

"I'm afraid that's the best I can do," said Stefan, dubiously surveying his handiwork, "but 'twill not last, as the wound still bleeds. We must have you to a leech as soon as possible, though what we are to tell Lord Markham I know not."

The duke opened his eyes. "Send for your groom from the stables. It must seem that he delivers a message for me and that I am required to return to Paris immediately. No more need be said. Lord Markham will not question my word, especially as you are to remain. I will, of course, take my leave as is proper, for I intend to return when the time is right. Would you also be so kind as to arrange for one of your lackeys to ride to Dieppe to intercept Oakes and send him to me at your hotel? I hope you don't mind my making use of your establishment once again, coz. I seem forever in your debt of late."

"Fustation," replied Stefan. "My home is yours. Maunders is the soul of discretion and can be relied upon to send for a physician. My valet will do all that is necessary for your departure, but we must be rid of the bloodstained towel and shirt. The safest thing is to consign them to the fire. As for your waistcoat, I will dispose of it later."

With some difficulty, the duke changed

into his traveling clothes while Stefan sent for his man from the stables. To make the ruse more convincing, he sealed a parchment from his writing case and addressed it to his cousin. Handing it to his bewildered groom, he bade him to deliver it to the duke's room in full view of Lady Markham, who was at that moment in the corridor, the good lady assuming that the groom had but gone to Stefan's room for the duke's direction.

Stefan's carriage was ordered immediately while the duke sought out Lord Markham to make his adieu, Lady Markham having informed him that her spouse was to be found in his usual retreat, the library. Stefan, accompanying his cousin, casually proffered his arm, which the duke gratefully made use of as if imparting some confidence, leaning heavily on the support as they descended the large staircase.

Entering the library, however, they found that his lordship was not alone. Both Julie and Bertram were cozily ensconced with their father by the fire, enjoying an amusing account of the day. As the cousins entered, Bertram sprang to his feet with an invitation that they should join the family group, but the words died on his lips as he saw that the duke was dressed for departure.

Drawing the folds of his fur-lined traveling cloak across his chest, the duke stood erect in the doorway. "I'm afraid I must return to Paris immediately," he drawled. "An urgent matter that needs my attention," and he vaguely indicated the parchment in his hand.

"Nothing serious, I hope," asked his lordship, coming to meet him full of concern.

"An irksome matter, no more," replied his grace, conscious now that Julie was watching him intently, a puzzled expression on her face. "May I make so bold as to ask you to keep Satanas for me until I can make proper arrangements for his stabling at Hôtel Blake? I'm afraid my house is under covers at the moment, as I have had no time to arrange otherwise, but I will make immediate arrangements for his housing as soon as I arrive in Paris."

"You will not be here for the Grand Ball on New Year's Eve?" asked Julie softly, coming forward and speaking for the first time, her large blue eyes searching the duke's face, sensing rather than seeing that something was amiss.

Turning to her, the duke's gaze softened, but the strain was visible about his lips. "I think not," he said softly, "but have no fear, I will return as soon as possible." Then, as if suddenly aware of the others: "Your forgiveness, but I must away before the light fails, as I am bound to reach Paris this night." For a moment longer his gaze held Julie's, and then, turning on his heel, he made his way into the hall, where lackeys were already lighting the candles in the sconces, casting a pool of light across the marble floor.

"Have no fear for Satanas," said Bertram, following him. "He will be well cared for, I promise you. My groom has treated him with a healthy respect since you took the handling of him."

"Of that I have no doubt," replied his grace. "He is an animal to command respect. You showed you have a fine choice in horseflesh, my boy."

"Fie sir, you will puff the young scamp up with his own importance," said his lordship, laughing as his son flushed with pleasure. "I have spent a week or more remonstrating on his lack of sense."

Lady Markham now joined the group in the hallway and lightly slipped her arm about her daughter's waist, but Julie's gaze remained riveted on the duke, noting the pallor of the face she held so dear, wondering what on earth could be wrong.

His lordship tried to delay the duke's

departure till morning, but Stefan interceded, saying that the coach was ready and at the door.

His grace thanked Lord Markham for his hospitality, returned Bertram's zealous handshake, and lightly kissed the hand proffered by her ladyship. Turning to Julie, he raised her slight fingers to his lips, lingering a moment longer than was necessary over the caress. Lord and Lady Markham exchanged a knowing glance, with only Julie noting the slight stiffness of his bow and the effort it cost him.

A few moments later, he was sinking thankfully back onto the velvet squabs in the darkened interior of Stefan's coach. The trees flitting past the windows were but shadows as the coachman sprang the horses. The jolting of the coach, which although well sprung was unavoidable, caused the duke no small amount of discomfort, but at least now he could drop all pretexts, and, closing his eyes, he suffered the discomforts as best he might.

Maunders was as reliable as Stefan had predicted. No sooner had the duke alighted from the coach and entered his cousin's house to stand somewhat unsteadily in its small, well-lit hall, than the worthy retainer had taken full stock of the situation. At the duke's curt explanation, he wasted no time in sending the whole household into action. M. Dubret, the physician, was immediately called while the duke's bedroom was made ready. Maunders himself aided his grace to his chamber and assisted him abed.

As the duke sank gratefully back against the bank of white pillows, Maunders smoothed the covers to add to his comfort, saying, with a reassuring smile, "Unless I am much mistaken, your grace, a glass of brandy is now what is needed."

"My very need," agreed the duke. " 'Twould certainly not go amiss, for I am chilled to the bone."

Maunders stirred the large log fire into roaring flames of orange and gold before procuring a decanter and glass from the library. Pouring a good measure, he was gratified to see that it helped restore some of his grace's former color.

Choosing this exact moment to arrive, M. Dubret frowned heavily at the reviving spirits, but deemed it better to say naught. He was a small, dapper man of about fifty who sported a heavily powdered bagwig. Large, bushy brows shadowed a pair of keen eyes that immediately appraised the situation, and with a sigh, he set about examining his patient. He made no comment on the fact that the wound had obviously been made by a sword, a fact that he was willing to overlook, considering the large fee he was sure the English duc was prepared to pay, and the doctor remonstrated only lightly that he should have been sought earlier, as M. le Duc was now so much weaker. After attending to the wound, M. Dubret stated that a few days abed would soon put it right and, should a fever start, he assured the duke he would be prepared to bleed him immediately, using only the finest of leeches.

All this the duke suffered in silence, mentally consigning his tormentor to the devil and suffering M. Dubret's ministrations with as much fortitude as he could muster in his present state of fatigue. Reluctantly, he had to admit that the salve the doctor used on the wound and the ill-tasting draught he administered from a violet-colored phial had made his grace feel a deal more comfortable. Although Stefan had made every effort to assure his cousin's comfort, he found that the doctor's dressing relieved some of the pressure from the wound.

Finally, proclaiming the duke to be well repaired, and stating his firm intention of returning on the morrow, M. Dubret made his departure, leaving full instructions with Maunders to cover any eventuality should such a personage as M. le Duc appear to suffer a relapse. The duke heaved a sigh of relief as the doctor finally closed the bedroom door, although his voice could be heard as he slowly descended the stairs, informing Maunders that his grace should be served nothing more than gruel for the next few days in case of a fever. The duke, meanwhile, made a mental note to throw any gruel offered him on the morrow at the good doctor's head.

When Marcel succumbed to the deep slumber of exhaustion, Maunders took up his post on a truckle bed that had been made up for him in the dressing room. Leaving the adjoining door fully open, he ensured that he would be instantly aware should the duke have need of him during the night.

New Year's Day dawned bleak, or so it seemed to the duke, who was taking a late breakfast, much against M. Dubret's instructions, in Stefan's breakfast parlor. A meal consisting of cold meats remained untouched on the large table as his grace sat clad only in breeches, shirt, and dressing gown, apparently absorbed in the patterns of the roaring fire. His wound was healing well, which was more than could be said of his temper. Left alone with his thoughts, he fared not so well. Sitting at the head of the table, negligently crossing his legs before him, he pursued his fruitless occupation, mindless of the lackey waiting in attendance a small distance behind his chair. A glass of canary, which a few days earlier he would have rejected at such an early hour, sat close at hand, his mood turning to the morose.

For almost an hour he sat thus, until the mantel clock chiming noon brought him from his reverie and, straightening in his chair, he ordered the lackey to remove the covers, he himself repairing to the library.

The room was chill, but the duke seemed not to notice. Instead, he stood surveying the graying sky through the large casement as the first few flakes of snow began to fall, perfectly suiting his mood. After a cautious scratching on the door, Maunders entered, chiding his grace for not returning to his bedchamber as M. Dubret had ordered. Encountering a cold stare for his remonstrations, Maunders suggested that a fire should be made up and a more comfortable chair be brought for his grace's ease.

The duke seemed somewhat indifferent but gave his consent by a slight inclination of his head, and immediately the room was filled with lackeys bringing hot coals from the nether regions to set a blaze and a large chair to place beside the hearth, a wide tapestry screen being unfolded and put as a shield from any draught between the door and chair.

Impatient of Maunders' ministrations, the duke dismissed the man and threw aside the woolen rug Maunders had spread over his knees. To all intents and purposes, his strength had fully returned, but Maunders and Dubret would insist on coddling him, a fact that irritated him greatly. He wished nothing more than to be left alone.

After several attempts at reading one of Stefan's finely tooled volumes, he negligently threw it aside onto a small, round table placed at his elbow. He sighed heavily, the frustration of his enforced inactivity almost impossible to bear. He was now fully prepared to admit that his affection for Julie was more than just a passing fancy. If truth be told, he loved her, an emotion that so far had eluded him and one that he found not to be as comfortable as one was led to believe. Julie had taken him completely unawares, captivating him from the start. Realizing now that he had loved her since the ball on Christmas Eve, he cursed himself for a fool for in no way attempting to fix her affections. Thoughts of what would be her reaction when his reputation became known to her proved most unwelcome, and, for the first time in his life, he was unsure.

Tossing back yet another glass of canary, he snapped the empty glass back into place on the table and, deciding that what he now needed was some diversion of thought, promised himself the dubious pleasure of visiting one of the gaming establishments sometime in the not-too-distant future.

Cautiously, the library door was opened, but not so quietly as to escape the duke's notice. "What the deuce is to do now?" he barked impatiently, once more preparing to fill his glass from the crystal decanter.

"Thought you might be asleep, coz," said Stefan with a grin, appearing from behind the screen. Then, raising his quizzing glass, he surveyed the decanter. "Never known you to imbibe this early in the day, Marcel. Pain that bad?"

The frown lifted from the duke's countenance. "My dear Stefan, you have no idea how pleased I am to see you. I am sorely in need of company other than my own. But what brings you here?"

"I'm afraid 'twas I," came a small voice from behind the screen, and slowly Julie, enveloped in a large traveling cloak of brown velvet sprinkled lightly with snow, entered the room in Stefan's wake. Seeing the duke about to rise, with satin skirts swishing, she came quickly forward to lay a restraining hand on his shoulder.

His face dark with anger, Marcel rounded on Stefan. "You fool," he expostulated. "Have you not more sense than to bring her here, unchaperoned, to a bachelor's house? She will be ruined!"

Stefan recoiled before his cousin's wrath. "Not my fault, Marcel. Said she'd come on her own if I didn't bring her. Thought it was safer for her to have an escort, so I agreed."

"Please don't be angry," she pleaded, catching at the duke's sleeve. "It was all my doing. I made Stefan tell me what had happened. I knew something was amiss when you left. You looked so drawn, but he would not tell me until I threatened to come here alone." Amid billowing skirts she dropped to her knees beside the duke's chair and, giving a slight sob, laid her cheek against his hand.

"Think I'll just have a word with Maunders," said Stefan, attempting tact, and he rapidly disappeared from the room and securely closed the door behind him.

It was a moment before the duke could speak, his anger having completely evaporated; in its place, a faint ray of hope spread through his being. Placing his free hand under Julie's chin, he raised her head, the hood of her cloak falling back to reveal a tearstained face now upraised to his.

"Don't cry, *mignonne*," he said softly.

"But 'tis all my fault," she said, weeping, fresh tears glistening on her lashes and slowly making their way down her cheeks.

"Nonsense, *mon cher*. Coustellet and I had a score to settle, nothing more," and then a little cruelly: "Do you weep for him also?"

"Sir," she flashed through her tears, "you know me not! Would I be here if I had any thought for him?"

"I only tease you, sweetheart," he said softly, and, placing his arm about her shoulders, he drew her head to rest against his chest, lightly brushing his lips against her tousled curls. "You should not have come. My wound was but slight. Stefan had no right to tell you, a fact I shall not easily forget."

Julie slowly pulled away. "Don't blame Stefan. I would have come last night had it not been for the ball. He stopped me by promising to bring me to see you today.

160

Mama thinks me at the manteau makers, so I cannot stay long, but I needed to reassure myself that you would be well. How I wish you had told me of your intention! Perhaps I could have persuaded you against it," and gently her fingers fluttered lightly over the bandage visible above the opening of the duke's shirt. "I shall never forgive myself."

Catching her hand to his lips, he pressed a caress against her palm. "You should not worry about me, *ma chère*. It is not right," and for a moment he resisted the temptation to kiss away her tears, afraid lest she be put to flight as before. His resolve could not stay firm, however, and gently drawing her once more to him he tenderly kissed her cheek. Finding no resistance, he sought her lips, rejoicing that she returned the favor. As his arms tightened about her, she slipped her own about his neck. Suddenly, as if by thought, she drew away, and he dropped his hold immediately, not wishing to frighten her.

Averting her face, she quickly rose and would have run from the room if he had not as quickly risen from the chair and caught her hand, detaining her. Standing now before her, he tried to make her look at him, but she hid her face against his shoulder, making only muffled sounds into the folds of his dressing gown.

"My love, forgive me," he said softly. "I meant not to frighten you. I was mistaken. It is too soon. I would give you more time."

To his surprise she gave a tearful chuckle. "Marcel," she said, now raising her eyes to his. "I wonder what you now think of me, to more or less force myself upon you. I should not have come, but, oh, I did so want to. I needed to be reassured."

Relief flooded him, and with a teasing light in his eyes he said, "If I were to tell you, love, exactly what I think of you, it would bring a blush to your cheek. But on reflection, I have always suspected you of a forwardness, a fact in which today I rejoice, for without your company I had become morose. I had come so to rely on it."

"Now you laugh at me," she chided, "but I am glad, for I feared greatly for you."

The duke drew her once more gently to him, and she was content to remain there. Then as he tenderly kissed her brow, he asked softly, "Could you love me, *mignonne?*"

She answered him by shyly placing her hands on his face to draw it down to her own and gently returning his kiss.

At that moment, Stefan knocked urgently at the door and without waiting for an answer entered unceremoniously, noting with some satisfaction how Julie still stood within the circle of his cousin's arm. Perhaps now he would be allowed some peace. "The snow is getting heavier," he said. "We must start back to Sefron immediately. My apologies, Marcel, but I must get Julie back while the roads are passable."

The duke was not enraged by the interruption, as his cousin feared. He had had his answer, and there would be plenty of time for both of them later. Now, the main concern was Julie's safety. "You must go now with Stefan, *mignonne*," he said, pulling her cloak warmly about her. "All will be well. I will come to you as soon as I am able."

Julie stole a small hand into his, saying nothing but holding tightly to his fingers as they walked to the door, where a lackey waited to help her into the carriage. There was only time for a brief *au revoir* before the front door was flung open, admitting a flurry of crystal-like flakes, and, with a quick flutter of her hand, she was gone, leaving the hallway feeling strangely empty.

Never in the whole of his life had the duke's mood and fortune taken such a complete turnabout. He was even prepared to suffer M. Dubret's ministrations with something like cheerfulness when the worthy doctor trudged through the snow some few hours later to inquire after his esteemed patient's health. The doctor, on seeing his patient so much improved, was even moved to say that the duke would soon be able to dispense with his services.

It was late in the evening and the duke was contemplating retiring to his bedchamber when the royal messenger arrived. His urgent summons on the front door had the effect of startling the young footman found to be almost dozing at his post and caused no small amount of curiosity among the lackeys. His entry into the hall, accompanied as it was by much foot stamping to rid himself of the snow that still clung to his boots, roused even the duke from his pleasant reverie and caused him to look enquiringly toward the library door. Maunders scratched lightly before entering, proudly bearing the missive, complete with royal seal, on a small silver salver.

"A message from King George, I believe, your grace," he said, bowing slightly and proffering the tray.

The duke raised a quizzical brow. It had been almost two months since he had last attended court, and he wondered for what reason he should now receive a missive, especially one that should be so urgent as to send a messenger across the channel in his wake. Taking the heavily embossed parchment from the salver, he bade Maunders to make arrangements for the courier's refreshment and overnight accommodation while bidding him to first bring a large branch of candles from the mantel for a better light.

When alone, the duke unhurriedly broke the red wax bearing the king's seal and spreading wide the parchment began to read the royally dictated *communiqué*.

CHAPTER TEN

Slowly the letter dropped from his hand and lay face upward at his feet, and the duke's countenance took on a stonelike quality. The news of Sir Lawrence's death affected him almost as a physical blow. The reason for his retreat to Paris had eluded him over the past few days, his thoughts being now channeled in a totally different direction, and to be brought back to reality so forcibly had shaken his very foundation.

He had not intended to kill the youth, only to teach him a lesson, a lesson that pride would not let him forgo. Also with the news of Lawrence's death came a royal command. King George and his wife were ill pleased, dueling as such being frowned upon among their familiars, and that one should result in a fatality was totally unacceptable. The royal missive now lying abandoned upon the hearth lamented not only the duel, but also the duke's whole life style, for which he had gained a deplorable reputation. A reputation, in view of the past ten days' happenings, he wished wholeheartedly he could revoke. King George, therefore, had decided that it was beholden to the Crown that his grace should marry, hoping this would prove to be a steadying influence upon his hitherto rake-shame existence. The queen herself, having made a suitable choice from among her ladies in waiting, awaited only the duke to pay the lady formal court. The missive also contained a scarcely veiled threat that should he fail to comply with the royal wishes, his presence at court would be considered an embarrassment and all privileges would be withdrawn.

The duke sat for some time, the only sound the steady ticking of the mantel clock as almost an hour sped by. So intense was his reverie that not even by as much as a flicker did he show himself to be aware of his surroundings. Thoughts tumbled through his mind, each jostling for supremacy. The phrase *if only* repeated itself countless times as he watched the flames die unattended in the hearth. He had fought many duels; how was he to have known that this particular one would threaten his whole existence as had no other? How could he now go to Julie with this on his conscience and ask her to be his wife, as he had intended? He put aside the thought of a bride chosen by the Crown. This could be amended by informing them of his own choice, one that he was sure they would wholeheartedly approve of, but to go to Julie with his hands soiled with Lawrence's death was almost unthinkable. He said *almost,* for he still held a ray of hope. If she should know nothing of it, could he in all conscience hide it from her? A small voice at the back of his brain said yes; while common sense warned him *beware.* A plan was fast forming in his mind, one that would not be put aside. If they should marry and he secured her affections, perhaps then he would find a way of proving himself to her before she should become aware of his past, hoping that by then at least he would have some chance of her forgiving him. It was a selfish plan, without a doubt; it was a foolish plan, but his heart would not listen to reason. Reason played no part when his entire happiness, indeed his whole future, was in jeopardy.

The more he thought, the more his mind returned to this, until, as the fire completely died away, he was firm in the conviction that if he were to have any hope of attaching Julie's life to his own, this was what he must do. Julie represented all he held dear. Believing her to be his salvation, he must put aside all thoughts of Lawrence's death. It was something he would face in the future if the occasion should arise; as for now, he must reply to the king as quickly as possible, informing him of his own marital intentions.

On this resolve, he rose and, taking the branch of candles from the table beside him, crossed to the escritoire. Seating himself, he took a sheet of fine white parchment and sharpened a quill. It took only a few moments to compose a reply, finding in its composition conviction in his resolve to have Julie at all costs, even if she should later cast him off. Folding the parchment and fastening it with his seal, he pulled the bell to summon Maunders, who, when he entered, was more than a little concerned at the fatigue that showed in the duke's whole being.

"Give this to the messenger immediately," said the duke, handing the letter to Maunders. "He shall rest here tonight, but make it clear that I expect him to set out for London at first light."

"It shall be as you wish, your grace," said Maunders. Then, unable to forgo his concern, with a familiarity born of long association, he said, "It has grown quite chill, sir.

Will you not return to your room? You must not overtax your strength."

For once, the duke complied without further ado, his thoughts lying heavy on his tired shoulders.

CHAPTER ELEVEN

By noon the next day, the snow had stopped and a wintry sun managed to cast its faint rays upon the white streets. The duke was still abed, Maunders having deemed it best not to wake him at his usual early hour after the exertions of the previous evening. It was then quite unexpected that a hired coach should be halted in the courtyard and a very weary Oakes alight, clutching in his arms a speckled pointer pup well wrapped in the folds of his traveling cloak. As Oakes gingerly picked his way over the snow, fearful lest he should lose his footing on the slippery surface, the pup wriggled but was firmly held against his side by a restraining arm. His journey had not been an easy one, as could be seen by the ravaged look on his already sour countenance. He had no great liking for animals, and the care of the pup had considerably added to the discomforts of the trip. It was a very bewildered lackey who admitted him into the hallway and dumbly accepted the small bundle that was thrust, shivering, into his arms.

Oakes, being only too glad to part with his tormentor of the past week, silently cursed the dog for all the trouble she had caused, and vainly tried to remove her hairs from his fine wool coat. A very haughty Maunders greeted Oakes, showing him into an office in the nether regions, begging him to be seated, and wasting no time in apprising him of the duke's condition, stressing the necessity for complete rest.

Showing not the slightest surprise at what had occurred in his absence, Oakes made it quite clear that now he was returned, he would take complete charge of his master, jealous lest anyone should try to usurp his position. Hearing the duke's bell ringing in the servants' hall, Maunders made to answer, but, placing a restraining hand on his arm and casting a meaningful look in his direction, Oakes forestalled him, now deeming it his place to look to his master.

Some short while later, the duke, once more seated in the library, awaited Oakes, who at his request had gone to fetch the pup from the kitchen, where she had been fed and was now cozily asleep before the fire. His grace looked a deal better than his restless night would have supposed, and his humor was fully returned now that he had finally reached his decision and was eager to carry it through. Oakes entered quietly, holding the small bundle in his arms.

"Bring her to me," commanded the duke. "Stand her here on the hearth before the fire. She appears to feel the cold."

Oakes did as he was bid, dropping to one knee and placing his tormentor at the duke's feet.

"A good choice," approved his grace, surveying the puppy through his quizzing glass. "Even though you think I served you ill by sending you back across the Channel, you have done well, my friend. You need not look at me with such a jaundiced eye. You will be well rewarded. Now, tell me, have I not fared well in your absence? I think you will find I have managed quite creditably, despite your belief that I could not do without your ministrations."

"I never doubted your grace," replied Oakes with an air of one greatly offended, for had not his master proved that very point only a few minutes before by insisting that he dress himself, a task that Oakes had lovingly performed these past ten years or more?

"Come now, don't be so sour," said the duke with a chuckle. "In your absence, I had need to become more self-sufficient, but now you are returned, I shall willingly give myself over to your attentions once more." Then in a rallying tone: "Now what shall we call the pup, for she shall have a name?"

"I have not thought, your grace," Oakes replied, watching with some distaste as the duke, somewhat stiffly, lifted the affectionate animal onto his knee. "May I remind your grace that you are wearing your new gray superfine, and that animal hairs are almost impossible to remove."

"I see your journey has done naught to quell your impudence," remonstrated the duke. "I have told you before, Oakes, I will not be dictated to. Now come, make an effort. We must find a name for the duchess here."

"I think that suits her quite well," replied a somewhat mollified Oakes. "In fact, sir, a worthy name."

"Aye, I think you have the right of it. Duchess it shall be — a Duchess for my duchess!"

"Shall I take her back to the kitchen, your grace?" asked Oakes, preparing to remove the pup from the duke's lap.

"No, leave her with me for a while. She presents a diversion. But tomorrow, if the roads are passable, I will take her to Sefron. She is a gift for Miss Markham. Now go, you seem sorely in need of rest. Perhaps then your countenance will not be so dour when I have need of you."

A grateful Oakes beat a hasty retreat, thankful at last to be able to relax his vigilance over so lively a charge.

Left alone, the duke grew impatient, watching the snow through the window overlooking the courtyard for any signs of a thaw. "Let us pray, my friend," he said, addressing the pup as she lay almost asleep on his knee, "that we are able to make the journey tomorrow, for I was never a patient man, and once having set my mind to something, I find delay irksome to the extreme. Let us hope your new mistress is awaiting my return as eagerly as am I. She knows not of your coming. I wonder what she will make of you."

Duchess moved her head to a slightly more comfortable position, lazily licking the slender hand that caressed her with her small, warm tongue. Here at last was someone who understood her, and she was content.

The duke rested his head against the back

of the chair, his legs stretched to the hearth. *Royal messengers be damned,* he thought, allowing his eyelids to lower over dreamy eyes. And so sat the pair in a world of their own until it was time for M. Dubret's visit.

This worthy gentleman, upon being apprised of the duke's intention to travel to the country on the morrow, cast up reproving hands, but his patient would have none of it. Stating that his wound was healing well, his grace made it known that he would no longer need the services of a physician. M. Dubret, reluctant to let so eminent a personage slip from his grasp, was nevertheless forced to agree that the duke had made a remarkable recovery, a fact that he attributed to his own doctoring skills and the duke's ironlike constitution!

On the morrow, determined not to be shaken from his purpose, the duke set out for Sefron at an unfashionably early hour, with Duchess dozing contentedly in a wicker hamper set at his feet. Sitting in the corner of the chaise, wrapped in a fur-lined traveling cloak, he waited impatiently as the team of four made what speed it could in the fast-forming slush of the busy Paris streets.

Once free of the town, the snow became

firmer on the less frequented roads, affording the horses a better grip on its silvery surface. Even so, for safety's sake, they were forced to proceed at a maddeningly slow pace. It was, therefore, almost noon before Sefron's gates came into view, affording his grace some reward for his patience. His chest ached slightly but, for once in his life, apprehension drove all other thoughts from his mind.

When the chaise was halted before Sefron's door, a lackey ran down the shallow steps to help the duke alight, his grace handing Duchess complete with hamper into the servants' keeping until he could see Julie.

As he entered the hall, where a footman took his cloak and tricorn, Lord Markham almost burst out of the drawing room. "Saw your coach arrive, my boy," he said, vigorously shaking the duke's hand. "Your cousin is in the games room. I'll send someone to fetch him. He'll be devilishly pleased to see you. Do you stay?"

Disengaging his hand, the duke made a short bow and, ignoring his lordship's question, said, "I would prefer it if you let Stefan be for the moment, Jonathan. I have need to speak to you in private. A confidential matter, you understand. A matter that concerns only ourselves."

"But of course, of course," said his lordship, with a knowing twinkle, and, leading the way into the drawing room, he closed the door against all intruders.

CHAPTER TWELVE

The duke's return had not gone unnoticed. Julie had seen the chaise arrive from her sitting room window. As impatient for a thaw as had been the duke, she had scarce left her vantage point since her return to Sefron two days earlier. Now her vigilance had been rewarded, and at the sight of him her hands fluttered nervously to her flaming cheeks. Leaving her room, she ran the length of the gallery, catching her skirts in her haste, and reached the landing just in time to see the duke disappear into the drawing room with her father. Her thoughts were in turmoil and, not daring to voice what she hoped, she waited, clutching the banister for support for what seemed an eternity, eyes bright and heart pounding with anticipation.

Eventually, the drawing room door was thrown open with some force, and Lord Markham hurried out into the hall, his face wreathed in smiles. He was just about to mount the stairs when he spied his daughter on the landing. "Come down, child," he called, scarce able to contain his excitement. "Lear wants to see you. Now, don't be coy, none of your missish ways today. He has something to ask you, but I will let him speak for himself."

Slowly descending the stairs, Julie somewhat hesitantly entered the drawing room, leaving her father in the hall gleefully congratulating himself on what he considered an extremely propitious interview.

Closing the door, she stood for a moment with her back to it as if seeing anew the powerful figure standing on the hearth before her. "Your wound?" she almost whispered.

" 'Tis well, *mignonne*," replied the duke in deepened tones. " 'Tis of no import." For a moment there was a shyness between them; then slowly the duke opened his arms, and she ran to him, burying her face against his shoulder, her dusky curls caressing his cheek.

"Did I do right to return, sweetheart?" he asked softly as, slipping his arm about her waist, he drew her to sit beside him on the couch.

"I have waited for your return. Need you

doubt it?" she replied, smiling up at him.

"I must be sure," he said, searching the sweet face turned toward him. "Your father has given me permission to pay you formal address, my love, but 'tis for you to say, not he. Will you have me, Julie, or do I speak too soon? Tell me now, for I swear I am not a patient man."

She chuckled softly. "Then I must teach you patience."

"You will not tease me, love," he said, playfully flicking her chin. "I shall have your answer, or you pay the consequence."

"Then I must have you, Marcel, for fear of your wrath," she said, smiling impishly and taking his hand to her cheek.

Catching her quickly to him, the duke fixed her well within his embrace, and it was some few moments before they drew apart. There was a smile in his eyes and a teasing tone in his voice when he said, "I can see you intend to lead me a merry dance, but be warned, I shall be a strict and jealous husband, lest you should grow tired and look elsewhere."

"Of that you need have no fear," she replied, of a sudden serious, slipping her hand into his to hold tightly to his fingers. "My heart is not lightly given."

"It is a gift of which I will take infinite

care," he said, reverently kissing her up-turned face. "I will leave for London on the morrow to put my estates in order. We will be married on my return."

"Must you go so soon?" she asked, disappointment heavy in her voice. "Could you not at least stay at Sefron until the snows are gone?"

"Alas, it is not possible. I have much to do, sweetheart, if I am to take a bride. I have my townhouse to prepare for your coming. Until now, it has of necessity been a bachelor's dwelling, but, now it is to have a mistress, all must be changed. I have also to visit Stovely, my country seat, to see what changes are needed there, for of recent years it has been little used. An occasional hunting party, no more. I, too, wish I could stay longer, but if I am to take a wife to England, there is much arranging to be done."

"How long will you be gone?"

"A few weeks, no more."

"It will seem an age," she said, disconsolate, a slight tremor sounding in her voice.

"Once I am returned, we will not be separated again. There will be no need," he promised, kissing her once more.

When he raised his head from the embrace, he surprised her by saying, "I am being remiss in my attentions, my love. I have a betrothal gift for you — not, as you may suppose, of jewels, but one I hope you will like equally well, and perhaps you will not be so lonely while I am away." Ringing the bell, he bade the lackey to bring in the hamper.

Julie watched in some amazement as the basket was set before her and, upon hearing a whimper and a short bark, was instantly on her knees. Once liberated, the jubilant occupant wasted no time in proving her relief at gaining freedom by rapturously repaying her benefactress.

"That, my dear, is Duchess," said the duke, taking in the happy scene before him. "A somewhat amorous creature, as you can see, proving a great trial to my valet on her journey over from England. I am persuaded, however, that with your guiding hand she will become a rewarding companion."

Julie knelt before him with Duchess in her arms. "You sent to England for her?" she asked, tears glistening on her lashes.

"She comes from my hunting box in Hertfordshire," said the duke, as he wiped away a tear from her cheek with his lace handkerchief. "Come, sweeting, I thought it would make you happy."

"But I am happy," she replied, with only

the smallest sniff. "How can I ever thank you?"

"I am afraid it is Oakes who deserves your thanks, not I, for it was he who braved the storms of the Channel and the discomforts of the highway — much, I may add, against his wishes. The poor fellow now lies abed nursing his aching limbs."

"Then I must send him a note of thanks," she said, chuckling.

"I pray you will not, my dear," said the duke. "He thinks himself a martyr in his master's cause, and to receive your thanks would wholly disillusion him!"

"Shame on you, sir," she said, her eyes twinkling. "You fool me not, and I see beneath that haughty exterior. You thought to replace Jasper, and I thank you."

"It is well, *mignonne*," the duke said softly. "I have reward enough. Your joy is all I need."

It was at this moment that his lordship, deeming it time the lovers were interrupted, gave a discreet tap on the door, entering with some caution. It needed only sight of his daughter's radiant countenance to confirm his hopes, and, as the duke rose to greet him, his lordship took his hand in a firm grip. "It is settled then," he approved, beaming. "My congratulations to you both.

184

Saw this coming days ago, my boy. Thought there was the makings of a match long before the two of you realized what you were at. Must warn you, though, it will of necessity be a quiet wedding here at Sefron's chapel, as Julie has not yet been presented at court."

"She shall be presented as the Duchess of Lear," said the duke, not without pride. Then, turning to Julie: "We will wed here, love, then for the honeymoon return to London, where you will be presented to the whole of society at the beginning of the season as my wife."

"But what of the engagement?" interrupted his lordship. "My wife and I had thought at least six months —"

"Have we need of an engagement, *chéri?*" asked the duke, taking Julie's hand in his. "I am impatient to have a wife."

"We will be married in March," she replied, returning the pressure of his fingers.

"It shall be as you wish," said his lordship, frowning slightly, "but why the haste?"

"As I have frequently said," replied the duke, smiling at his betrothed, "I am not a patient man!"

CHAPTER THIRTEEN

London in January was devoid of company, everyone aspiring to the haut-ton having repaired to the country, some to recoup their losses, others merely to rest in preparation for yet another hectic social season. To those considered in the know, however, the duke's return caused no small amount of comment and speculation. He was generally well liked among the ladies, his ramshackle reputation proving somewhat of a fascination, but fathers and husbands alike were wont to eye him askance. The story of the duel had proved something of a seven-day wonder among society, being proclaimed as an error of judgment on the duke's part and a foolhardy challenge on Lawrence's head, and in the weeks that had passed it had been superseded several times in the ranks of the gossips by even tastier scandals.

Hearing of the duke's return, the king lost no time in summoning him to his presence, receiving him alone and not in the best of humors, showing that he was still ill pleased with what he termed a deplorable affair. After giving full vent to his anger at the beginning of the interview, however, his mood mellowed considerably on hearing of the projected match, taking such a complete turnabout as to move him to promise the duke high favors within the royal household to show his approval of the marriage. All this the duke forbore with great fortitude. Knowing the vagaries of the king's moods, he held no great hopes of the promised position; indeed, he had no desire for courtly favors. He was, however, now fully assured of the Crown's forgiveness.

Lord Markham had surpassed himself in his preparations for his daughter's wedding. Although the ceremony itself had been for the immediate family only (a fact for which the bride and groom were thankful), Sefron's portals now held almost three hundred guests, who had just risen from a magnificent banquet set in the couple's honor — upward of sixty dishes set over eleven courses. It was generally agreed among the established members of society that the bride and groom, as they stood now in the large ballroom accepting congratulations and well wishes, presented a perfectly matched pair. Indeed, several ladies of sentiment were heard to utter a scarcely suppressed sigh upon perceiving the couple's happiness and the obvious pride the duke showed in his new bride.

With her hand lightly resting upon the duke's arm, Julie stood at his side, radiant in a gown of heavy cream brocade spread over wide panniers. French lace foamed at her shoulders and breast and cascaded from the petticoat she wore beneath. Pearls adorned her ears and slender neck and were sewn into intricate patterns on her bodice. "Pearls are for tears, love," her mother had warned, but Julie had dismissed this as a foolish superstition, and rightly so, she thought, gazing at the duke. He was at his most amiable and resplendent in cloth of silver. Sapphires and diamonds twinkled among the Melchin lace at his throat and blazed on the order he wore across his chest, repeating themselves on the garters at his knees and the buckles of his shoes.

Throughout the long day they had scarce time for a word with each other. Indeed, it seemed that they had never been left alone since the duke's return from London, Julie forever being turned this way and that in preparations for her trousseau. The duke, however, in a hasty aside, had confided to his bride that they would stay the night at Hôtel Lear and then depart on the morrow for England, where he would be assured of his wife's undivided attention without the many interruptions he had suffered at the hands of her family over the last two weeks.

Lady Markham stood a small way from the happy couple, leaning on her husband's arm while ineffectually dabbing at the tears that would rise despite her resolve to stay firm. His lordship lightly remonstrated with her for being hen-witted but found it necessary to clear his throat several times himself before he could regain some of his former bluff.

For a moment, the press of guests lessened about the bride and groom and, taking the chance so opportunely offered, the duke drew Julie into a curtained alcove, immediately encircling her within his arms.

Smiling, he raised her left hand to admire her wedding ring, saying, "What think you now, madam wife?"

"I think, husband, that our absence will be remarked on," she replied, smiling and laying her hand against his cheek.

"Be that as it may, *mignonne,* I swear I will not return to the milling throng until I have a kiss," he vowed, holding her even closer and taking the favor before it could be denied him with an ardor belied by his humor.

"Fie on you, sir," Julie reproved, dimpling and peeping at him through lowered lashes in a way that captivated him. "We are now a married couple, and such open signs of affection are frowned upon by society."

"That, for society," he laughed, snapping his fingers. "I will have you away from here tonight, *chéri,* and then you will be at my mercy. Does that not terrify you?"

"Not a jot, sir," she replied, feigning haughty indifference. "In fact, sir, I must warn you that you have taken an extremely resourceful bride, and one who is not easily daunted!"

He chuckled and kissed her brow. "I see I must needs have my wits about me. It would seem that I have married a veritable termagant. Who would not pity me?"

"I, for one," said a voice behind him as Stefan, invading their privacy, stepped through the heavy curtain. "In truth, I would wish any bride well who could better you, coz!"

"The devil you would," said the duke with a laugh, reluctantly releasing Julie from within the circle of his arms. "I see you have no qualms in interrupting our *tête-à-tête.* A fact that at any other time would have compelled me to serve you a leveler, but not today. Today I am disposed to be magnanimous, for you will not have the opportunity to repeat your indiscretion once this hour is through."

Stefan grinned boyishly. "Knew you'd see it that way, Marcel, but I thought you might be persuaded to take a farewell drink before you leave, for I shall not see you again until I come to London at the end of the year."

The duke was about to refuse when Julie gave him a gentle push in the direction of the ballroom. Chuckling, she said, "Stefan has given me the very excuse I need to be rid of you while I change into something more suited to our journey. It would seem I have grown tired of my husband already."

"Imp," replied the duke, smiling indulgently. "I trust it will not become a habit for you to dismiss me so out of hand. I give you half an hour, no more, then we away."

"It will be as your grace wishes," she said in mock penitence, dropping a deep curtsy, her wide skirts billowing.

"Rogue," said the duke with a laugh, kissing her outstretched hand, "but I warn you, I shall have my revenge and it will be complete. You will not escape without consequence," and making a profound leg, he disappeared into the ballroom on Stefan's arm.

Still smiling, Julie was about to leave the alcove in his wake when a fashionable young woman dressed in green-spangled satin spread over extremely wide panniers made a sweeping entrance and gave a small startled cry at the sight of her. "Your grace must forgive me," she breathed, apparently overawed by the presence she now found herself to be in. "It was not my intention to interrupt you."

"You did not interrupt," replied Julie, smiling kindly. "I was just about to retire to my apartment to change," and so saying, she made to leave, but a bejeweled hand detained her.

"May I say how much I admire you, your grace," said the woman now eyeing her boldly. "I think you so very brave."

Julie, halted by this stranger, looked puzzled. "Brave? Why should I be thought to be brave, madam?"

The woman looked surprised. "But have you not married the Duke of Lear? That in itself needs courage."

Julie drew herself up to her full height. "I can assure you, there was no need of courage on my part," she said haughtily, twitching aside her skirts and once more prepar-

192

ing to leave, but again the hand detained her, holding fast to her wrist with an iron-like grip belied by the smallness of the stranger's fingers. "Who are you?" she demanded, attempting to free herself from the hold. "How dare you accost me in this manner?"

At the raising of Julie's voice, the stranger immediately relinquished her clasp. It would not suit her purpose should they be interrupted. Her smiling face distorted with a sneer as she replied, "You know me not, your grace, but I know of your marriage to the Duke of Lear."

"Obviously, or you would not be here," snapped Julie. "But I ask you again, why should I be in need of courage?"

"Why, to enter into this marriage of convenience, your grace, you must indeed be brave. It is the talk of London as to how the king has compelled the duke to seek a bride erstwhile all connections with the Crown would be severed. It is also general knowledge that now he has obliged the king by adhering to his wishes, and so quickly, too, that royal favors await him upon his return to England." With a sly look from beneath her lashes the stranger watched the effect her words had on Julie and a slow smile touched her lips as she saw the bride pale. "Could it be possible that you know nothing of this?" she asked, with a great show of innocence.

"Madam, I can assure you, you are mistaken. I would not lend myself to a contrived marriage. It is above everything I abhor. Your informant has misled you."

"Is it possible that your grace has been deceived — tricked, even?" said the woman, full of false concern. "Did you not know that a messenger arrived in Paris on New Year's Day with the command? Could it be that you know nothing of the duke's reason for coming to France in the first place?"

"New Year's Day?" repeated Julie stupidly. "You say the messenger arrived on New Year's Day, but that is impossible, that is the day when —"

"I do not lie, your grace," said the stranger with a sneer, folding her hands before her. "If you doubt me, ask your husband. I am sure he will be only too delighted to enlighten you."

"I do not believe you," cried Julie, pacing the floor. "I will call Marcel, and you will be forced to face him with your lies."

"Call him, by all means, and hear it from his own lips," purred the stranger recklessly, confident in her triumph. "No doubt he will be only too eager to tell you of the young

194

man he murdered in a mockery of a duel over a trollop at the Cyprian Hall that necessitated his immediate removal from England. Why else should he come to Paris in such haste? Ask any of the assembled company, my dear. They all know of his reputation as a rakehell. Could it be that you really are such an innocent that you have not also heard of his adventures among the so-called demimonde?"

"Madam," whispered Julie, clutching at a fold of the heavy curtain for support. "I tell you to your teeth, you lie. I know my husband has no fair reputation — I do not ask it of him. But what you say is untrue. I know not what motive you may have, save a wish to destroy me, but I tell you, you shall not succeed."

A maniacal gleam shone in the woman's eye. "The motive is not mine, your grace," she sneered. "I but carry the message for a mutual acquaintance who has no love for your husband, but I swear what I say is the truth. You think he loves you?"

"Yes!"

"Has he ever told you so? Do you not wonder at the haste of your marriage, the speed at which he returned to England once it was agreed?"

Stricken, Julie stood before the stranger,

her brain searching for an answer. She could not comprehend this woman and her accusations. Who was she to put such thoughts into her mind? Who was she to cast such doubts? Search her numbed memory as she would, she could not hear him say, "I love you." She had taken it for granted that her feelings were reciprocated when he had asked her to marry him, for why else should he show such tenderness? Why else should he court her affections? The answer came unbidden — to placate the king! Had he in truth tricked her into a marriage of convenience? This hurt more than the knowledge of the duel and his rakish reputation. Had he not, even for a little while, loved her, or was she merely a means to an end?

"I see, your grace, that I have given you food for thought," said the stranger, smiling sweetly and preparing to take her leave. "Perhaps you will now see why you will need courage. Ask your precious husband if I speak the truth. Ask him of Sir Lawrence's death. I am sure he will be only too pleased to enlighten you and furnish you with the details. I congratulate you on your marriage, madam, and wish you joy." Then suddenly flinging wide the curtain, she was gone, leaving only a heavy perfume behind her.

Stefan, at that moment going in search of

Bertram, saw the mysterious woman leaving the scene of her triumph with a catlike contentment on her classic features. It was to be seen by his sudden frown that he was not well pleased, and, stepping in her path, he sought to detain her. "I never thought to see you here, Caroline," he said, frowning. "I would have thought this to be the last place you would wish to show your face. How gained you entry?"

"My dear Stefan, as charming as ever," she said, tapping his cheek with her fan. "I assure you my entry was not forced. I had but to join the throng. My visit has been well worth the effort, I assure you."

"What mischief have you been at?" snapped Stefan, seeing Julie leaving the alcove in apparent haste to change. "I swear, wherever you choose to visit, there is always some mischief afoot."

"You credit me too well," said Lady Caroline. "I but wished to congratulate the happy couple."

"If you have said ought to upset Julie —"

"La, sir, what could be said?"

Stefan's eyed narrowed. "Knowing you, my dear, you would not look so well pleased unless something was afoot. By-the-bye, who has your protection now?"

"That, *mon ami,* is not now your concern,"

197

snapped Lady Caroline, twitching her skirts aside. "I am sure such a trivial matter will not interest you. Now, I will take my leave. The company bores me."

With a mocking bow, Stefan made way for her to pass, raising his quizzing glass, the better to view her exit.

Had he been privileged to witness her ladyship's departure from Sefron's portals, he would have been even more concerned for his cousin's happiness, for Caroline now entered a concealed coach bearing Coustellet's coat of arms. Within the shadowed interior, her protector had eagerly awaited her return, impatient to hear the results of her visit. Now, as he listened to the details of her brief encounter with the Duchess of Lear, his contentment grew, and he realized how complete would be his revenge and felt assured that his actions would spell destruction for his enemy. Of what worth His Grace, the Duke of Lear's marriage now? This was one blow from which he would not recover and that would last his life through. So much more rewarding than a physical assault.

The shadows of the mild spring evening had started to form as the duke and his duchess stepped into the chaise waiting at the foot of Sefron's sweeping steps. Guests overflowed onto the lawns and driveway as they wished the happy couple farewell, their laughter echoing as the coach and four sped down the drive and into the country lanes.

Alone at last in the darkened interior, the duke held Julie to him and, finding no response from her lips, kissed her brow. "Tired, sweetheart?" he asked softly. "It has been a long day. Come, lay your head against my shoulder. We have some two hours before we reach Paris and Hôtel Lear. Try to rest a little." Still finding the slender form beside him to be unyielding, he asked, slightly puzzled, "Is anything amiss, *mignonne?*"

Drawing away from his encircling arms, Julie sought the shadows of the corner, holding her cloak about her as if she found the evening air chill. The questions she would ask tumbled through her brain but could find no utterance, so all-consuming was the torment that enveloped her. Tears stung her eyes, and she longed for him to comfort her, but how could she tell him of the accusations that had been leveled against him? Suddenly, the moon appeared from behind the clouds and briefly illuminated the interior of the coach, its light lasting only long enough for the duke to perceive the stricken face beside him.

"What is wrong, sweetheart?" he asked, taking her hand to his lips and feeling the fingers tremble within his grasp. Then, as if trying to make light of it, he asked, "Do I frighten you so, love? Have no fear, I was but jesting and shall not play the heavy husband. I wish only to see you happy. You will not be coerced in any way."

At his words a half-strangled sob escaped her lips, her hands covering her face.

"Julie, tell me what is wrong," he pleaded, stretching out his arms to her and once more attempting to draw her to him. The look of trust had gone from her eyes. He felt its loss almost as a physical blow, and cold fingers clutched at his heart.

"I would ask you about Sir Lawrence," she said, raising a tearstained face to his, her eyes pleading for him to deny all knowledge of his existence.

As if taking a physical blow, the duke's arms dropped to his side and she saw his whole being stiffen. "So soon," he uttered in disbelief. "How come you to know?"

"That matters not," she replied, a calming numbness overtaking her, as if to dull the pain. "I must ask you this, my husband — did you receive a royal command from the king on New Year's Day, and was that command for you to wed?"

"There was a missive from the king," he said quietly, "but forswear, my love, I did not receive it till late evening. I had hoped to spare you from all details of Lawrence's death, but it would seem I have been forestalled. It is not a matter of which I am proud. I can but hope in time you will forgive me."

"But what of the command to wed?" she insisted.

" 'Twas of no import. I had already chosen my bride."

"Or more rightly, Marcel, was it then that you chose your bride? Could it be, my lord duke, that at the king's command, we have contracted a marriage of convenience?"

"What perverse nonsense is this?" asked the duke in disbelief. "No one should know better than you that this is no marriage of convenience, but a love match. I know not what manner of gossip to which you have been listening, but I say it is false."

"What then, sir, of your reputation?"

The duke froze; his world was crumbling before him. "It would seem my downfall is complete," he drawled, withdrawing into the aloofness he had abandoned so many weeks before. "Now, my dear, you see my true colors and may examine me for what I am.

I would hide all from you, but I find truth will out. I had hoped to have time to win you over before the truth should become known to you, therein seeking forgiveness, but it seems it is not to be. Obviously you are well informed of my former life, and I see by the stricken look you give me in what light you now view me. My apologies, madam. I should not have tried to steal my happiness at the cost of yours."

Still no words of love had he uttered, and Julie, sitting pathetically erect in the corner of the coach, whispered, "It would seem then, sir, that ours is indeed a contrived marriage." And slowly the joy of the day drifted into oblivion.

CHAPTER FOURTEEN

When the duke's carriage finally halted before the steps of Hôtel Blake, he waved aside the would-be attentions of the lackey who hurried forward from the house and flung wide the carriage door. Stepping down from the coach, his grace himself let down the steps and assisted his wife to descend. A welcoming light shone across the pavement, and Marcel could see that his servants had collected in the hall to welcome the bride and groom. He uttered an oath beneath his breath. Covertly, he examined his wife's pale countenance, and his heart clenched at the anguish he saw there. He would have spared her this.

Taking Julie's cold fingers in his, he placed her hand on his arm and led her forward, relieved that she did not rebel against his touch. It struck at his very core to see her so disconsolate, and he wished for nothing more than the privacy they were denied.

Coming forward to offer the congratulations of the staff, the majordomo informed his master that, as he had ordered, the bridal supper would be served in the small sitting room that connected the ducal bedchambers.

Pleading his wife's fatigue, Marcel led Julie through the line of servants and up the grand staircase to the first landing and, entering the sitting room, closed the door against all intruders.

He had expected tears and further recriminations, but Julie just stood in the center of the room, her cloak still about her shoulders, looking lost. He went to remove her cloak, but she shrank from his touch, and a layer of ice closed around his heart. He tried to force himself to feel nothing and was unprepared for the emotions that threatened to engulf him.

" 'Twould seem my touch repulses you, madam wife," he said, retreating behind the safety of hauteur. "Am I to remain damned in your eyes?"

Afraid that if she attempted to speak the tears would come in torrents, Julie remained silent, only the pain in her eyes telling of her anguish.

A discreet tap came on one of the bedroom doors, and a lady's maid, who had been sent to Hôtel Blake earlier in the day, came hesitantly into the room. Dropping a curtsy, she went to remove her mistress' cloak.

"Leave us," commanded the duke in an awful voice.

The maid looked terrified and turned immediately to leave the room, but Julie, thankful for the chance to escape her husband's presence, seized the opportunity and hastily followed in her wake, closing the door securely behind her.

Still the tears did not come. Her anguish was too deep for tears. Instead, curled in her lonely bed, Julie felt her despair almost as a physical pain. He had not denied the duel. He had not denied the royal decree. Could she believe anything he had told her? It would seem not. He was a man of his time, and she expected not a spotless reputation, but in her naïveté, she had not been prepared for the reality of his life. To hear her informant describe him as a rakehell and murderer had devastated her, and she realized how little she knew of his world.

When the coach drew away from Hôtel Blake the following morning, it was obvious that neither Marcel nor Julie had slept the previous night. Marcel had planned a leisurely journey to the coast but now ordered that they reach their destination as quickly as possible.

The ensuing week was at a direct variance to what either had envisaged, each treating the other with an awful civility. The journey to London seemed overlong, with scarce a word being spoken. Had but the duke overridden Julie's accusations and fears, he would have easily found forgiveness, but as the days passed, so did the opportunity, each becoming a stranger to the other. The duke, thinking his bride to be repulsed by her findings and not realizing their origin or to what proportions they had been made, thought it useless to utter protestations of love, for what delicately bred female would not be disgusted at such revelations? Each in their own way found the other to be unapproachable. Even the arrival of Duchess at Blake House a few weeks later did not have the power to raise her mistress' spirits.

London welcomed Her Grace, the Duchess of Lear with open arms. Her entrée into society was a marked success, and who noticed if the newly married couple were not forever in each other's pockets, for so was the fashion.

For Julie's first excursion to the opera, however, the duke insisted that she accept his escort and arranged an unexceptional party to include Lord and Lady Steins, distant relatives of his.

The box, which had been rented for the season on the duke's behalf by his secretary, commanded not only an uninterrupted view of the stage but also allowed its occupants to see and be seen by other members of the audience. Julie sat at her husband's side, her eyes bright with anticipation. Impatient for the commencement of the evening's entertainment, she eagerly awaited the raising of the curtain.

The candles in the auditorium cast a soft glow over her countenance, making her lovelier than ever, thought the duke bitterly, as, in an attempt to divert his thoughts, he entered into a marked conversation with Lord Steins.

As the curtain rose, Julie sat eagerly forward, resting her hand of the rim of the balcony. The duke retreated slightly into the shadows, the better to observe without being observed, his eyes never leaving his wife's face. Choosing a gown of rose silk, Julie had dressed with great care. Her dusky curls, fashionably powdered, were confined over her left ear with a diamond clip. Diamonds sparkled on her breast, as she wore the famous Lear necklace, and hung in droplets from her delicate ears. The duke caught his breath at the picture she presented and for the hundredth time cursed himself for being a fool.

At the end of the first act, Julie, momentarily forgetting their rift, turned eagerly toward him. "Was that not magnificent, Marcel?" she breathed. "I had never thought to hear such voices."

"I am afraid, my love, as is common with most males, I fail to be acquainted with the opera's finer points," he replied, smiling ruefully. "Perhaps you can teach me to appreciate the art?"

"I believe it to be something of an acquired taste," interposed Lord Steins. "I myself have no great liking for it, either, but come to please my wife."

"That, my dear, is perfectly untrue," chuckled Lady Steins. "You have never done anything solely to please me in your life. Confess, you have a secret passion for the stage, in any shape or form. Why, only last week you dragged me to that dreadful farce at Drury Lane. I was so bored I started counting heads."

Amid the following laughter, the curtain of the box was put aside and a young gallant of some considerable address entered. At sight of him, Julie gave a squeak of delight and, hastily rising, threw herself into his arms. "John," she cried. "I never thought to see you here, but of course you must have returned for the season."

Taken somewhat by surprise, the duke raised his quizzing glass, the better to observe this young gentleman who so obviously warranted his wife's enthusiasm. His eyes flicked over the chestnut hair worn unpowdered and the regular features, finally coming to rest on the sober suit of charcoal velvet, its cut proclaiming a master's hand, and on the instant he took an unwarranted dislike to John.

Turning to the duke, Julie said, "May I make known to you my cousin John? I had thought him still to be at Oxley, his country seat. You have no idea how pleased I am to see him."

Slowly the duke rose to greet the newcomer, and Sir John Austin gave a short bow. "I had heard my cousin had wed," he said soberly. "My congratulations, my lord duke. You must know that I once held hopes in that direction, but she would have none of me. You, sir, have obviously succeeded where I failed."

"Fie on you, John," chided Julie lightly. "Why so dour? You must know we would not deal at all well together. I am not at all the kind of wife you would wish for, as you were forever chiding me on my levity."

"Aye, 'tis true," relented Sir John, smiling down at her, "but I still hold you in some affection. Quite cousinly, of course," he added, catching sight of the warning gleam in the duke's eye.

But his grace, feeling his nose to be put out of joint by his wife's rapturous reception of her cousin, was not to be mollified. Instead, proffering his seat to the unwelcome guest, he retreated to the rear of the box, finally entering the corridor in no even temper at the sight of them entering into a cozy *tête-à-tête*.

It was with some surprise that he found his perambulations halted by an elderly lady in an enormous ladder wig adorned with a profusion of ostrich feathers. Her overly painted face showed a wealth of character.

"Aunt Augusta," he said, bowing low over her parchmentlike hand. "What a delight it is to see you."

"Nonsense!" she snapped. "Don't try to bamboozle me. It don't suit you."

"Nothing of the sort," said the duke, feeling himself once more being reduced to the status of schoolboy. "But I swear I had never thought to meet you here of all places, Aunt."

"Humph," she replied, rapping his knuckles playfully with her fan. "Can't stand the place above the first act and only come to be seen. I'm on my way to Lady Margaret's. She's promised there will be high stakes tonight."

"Gambling as usual," said the duke with a grin. "I would have thought you to have run through your fortune by now."

Augusta gave an unladylike bark of laughter. "You young scamp. Have you no faith in my skill with the cards? But why are you out here instead of with that wife of yours? I see she has young Austin dancing attendance on her, and so soon after the wedding too."

"A fact I am well aware of," snapped the duke, once more returned to his ill humor.

"You can get off your high ropes with me," she countered haughtily. "I'm no Banbury babe. It don't take a crystal ball to tell all is not right between you. You're too lax with the chit. Bring her more to heel."

That his aunt had perceived the gulf between himself and Julie surprised the duke not at all, for throughout his life it would seem that Augusta had had amazing powers of perception. In fact, as a child he had often suspected her of being a witch, as not the slightest misdeed escaped her attention.

"The girl will take," she said. "Indeed, she is already being hailed as one of the season's beauties and as an original. I wish her well, Marcel. She's an engaging little thing. Met her at the Duchess of Rye's reception the other day, at which, by-the-bye, your absence was noted. Had quite a long coze with her, and although she confessed to nothing out of the ordinary, I could see that all was not right between you. Can't understand what ails the pair of you. Was led to believe it was a love match, and then here you are, acting as if you cared naught for each other."

"I believe you may have the right of it, Augusta. At least, it *was* a love match, until someone decided to apprise my new bride of my reputation and past indiscretions. Can you not wonder that she might be repulsed? Put yourself in her shoes. Would you wish me to husband?"

"Well, if that's all that stands in your way, you're a bigger fool than I gave you credit for, Marcel. Woo the chit! A man with your address should have no difficulty. Always had 'em falling at your feet. If you ask me, all you need do is storm her defenses. It's obvious the girl still has some affection for you."

"I think not, Aunt," he said, turning away. "You did not see the look of devastation on her face when she knew the rights of me, and who should blame her? Besides, she must come to me of her own accord. I will not be seen to pressure her."

"Do you love the chit?" asked Augusta, trying hard to read his averted countenance.

"You need ask?" he said, turning such a look of anguish upon her that she was left in no doubt.

"Then all I have to say is, *do* something about it. I'm a female, so I should know. In my younger day, I gave naught for any man who gave up without a fight. Can't stand a man without backbone, and that is something I never thought you lacked. *Woo the girl!*"

"You think it would serve?"

"I know so!"

"Then, madam, I bow to your superior knowledge."

"That's more like it," she said approvingly. "Now you may walk me to my carriage, for the second act started some ten minutes ago, and your wife will be wondering at your absence."

Considerably heartened by his conversation with Lady Augusta, the duke was able to return to his box with something quite like composure, even going so far as to magnanimously suggest that Sir John should join his supper party after the opera. Julie, applauding this suggestion, urged her cousin to accept, feeling that at last she had found a kindred spirit.

Several days sped by, and it would seem to the duke that every time he returned to Blake House from an expedition he was bound to meet Sir John, either just arriving or bidding his adieus. For a while, the duke strove to ignore the irritation this gentleman's presence caused him, even going so far as to attempt civility upon these chance encounters, but, after almost two weeks of Austin's continual attendance upon his wife, his grace's patience would forbear no more.

"Does that young pup intend to take up residence on my doorstep?" he snapped, entering Julie's sitting room just as Sir John had left. "It seems whatever time of day I return that I am forever tripping over him. Has he no home to go to?"

"He but bears me company," replied Julie, calmly taking up her embroidery and plying her needle with what he thought to be unnecessary care.

"I should not have thought you in need of company, my dear," retorted the duke haughtily, "especially with your diary so full. He even escorted you to the ball at Sturgis' last night."

"Would you prefer I went alone, sir?"

"My dear, you play your cards wrong if you suppose to catch me there. I offered you my escort, but you refused it. Make no bones about it, Julie, you prefer his company to mine."

Julie paled slightly but preserved her air of tranquility, which served all the more to inflame his temper. It was the first time they had spoken on such terms since their marriage, previously managing to keep their conversation quite impersonal.

"I would not say I prefer his company, Marcel, but I find him more approachable, more ready to listen to what I might have to say."

Contrite, he came to her, hand extended. "Then won't you talk to me now, love? I promise you will find me a most attentive listener. We had not used to be so distant."

The temptation was too great. Dropping the needlework to the floor in her haste, she rose and, ignoring the outstretched hand, moved away, saying, "La, sir, look at the time. I will be late, for I am engaged to dine at Lady Quinn's at seven."

"Why not dine with me this evening?" he asked casually, watching her from beneath lowered brows as he seemingly inspected the sapphire on his finger. "It would be novel, would it not, to spend an evening at home together?"

"I'm afraid that is impossible," she replied airily. "John is to call for me in an hour."

"Damn *John* to blazes," exploded the duke, flinging out of the room and slamming the door behind him.

A slow smile spread over Julie's pale countenance. Perhaps it would serve, after all; at last her husband had been shaken out of his aloofness.

CHAPTER FIFTEEN

As the season drew on, it soon became the rage to be included among the numbers invited to Blake House by the Duchess of Lear for the various entertainments she evolved. It was hardly surprising, therefore, that, as her husband usually found himself to be otherwise engaged on these occasions, she should collect a following among the male members of society, establishing, as it were, her own set. If it was seen that the young duchess seemed exceedingly gay, even the most stringent moralist was forced to admit that she was never seen to overstep the bounds of propriety. It *was* noted, however, that on these occasions, as indeed many others, Sir John Austin never strayed far from her side, ever ready to comply with her smallest wish or to lend his support to any scheme of her making. Julie received praise as something of a wit as well as a beauty, her address proclaiming her as an unusual.

Her mastery of the equestrian arts soon became apparent as, accompanied by Sir John, she took her place in Hyde Park, riding out on a mare of his choosing at the fashionable hour of four to five on any afternoon that proved itself suitable. Far from wooing his bride, and conscious in part of her desire to annoy him, the duke felt a great inclination to box her ears. Seeing her riding out on one of Sir John's horses, he remonstrated with himself for not having made provision for her to ride. Jealous of any office performed by another, and not wishing to admit to what extent the matter irked him, he resolved to find her a suitable mount.

Silently, Julie paced her bedroom floor, an anxious Duchess at her heels, wondering at her mistress' agitation. It was well after noon, the sun was shining, and surely her husband, for all there was a gulf between them, would not let her birthday go unmarked. She had breakfasted in her room, half afraid to face him across the breakfast table, lest her dejection should show. Taking her time over her toilette, she had heard him go out almost an hour ago.

Flowers and a charmingly wrapped package, which still remained unopened, had been promptly delivered from Sir John, and her sitting room was littered with greetings and similarly unopened gifts from her friends and admirers. Unfortunately, the only person she would wish remembrance from seemed totally oblivious of the occasion, and for as much as she told herself that it was childish to care, her eyes misted each time they rested upon the other gifts.

Slowly, the fingers of the mantel clock crept to two o'clock, Julie refusing the light nuncheon offered, the thought of food being obnoxious.

As the much-watched clock chimed half after two, her maid entered and, dropping a curtsy, delivered a note to her mistress. Recognizing the hand of the duke, Julie tore open the missive. Her mood not of the best, she read the bold script. The letter bade her to join her husband in his study and to attire herself for riding.

I will do nothing of the sort, she thought mulishly. *He shall not leave me alone half the day and then command me to attend him, obviously for some outing of his own arranging, without as much as a by-your-leave.* It was in this frame of mind that she left her apartments and, with a crispness in her step, made her way down the stairs and to the duke's study at the rear of the house.

Having some fair idea as to what her mood would be upon receiving so curt a missive, his grace awaited Julie's arrival with some amusement. Feeling himself to have the upper hand, he remained quite calm, confident in his ability to handle the situation.

Entering the study in much the same manner in which she had left her apartment, Julie thrust the note before him. "And what, may I ask, is the meaning of this?" she demanded, her face flushed with indignation.

"My dear, you are not dressed as I desired," remonstrated the duke mildly. "I must apologize if my missive was not quite clear on that point, but I particularly wished for you to wear your habit."

"I will do nothing of the kind," she snapped, an unreasoning anger rising. "I hear nothing from you all day, and then suddenly you decide, quite out of the ordinary way of things, that you wish my company. I tell you, sir, it will not do! Am I to await your pleasure?"

"I had no idea you were awaiting me," replied the duke silkily, unable to keep a slight tremor of amusement from his voice. "I had supposed you to have gone on some expedition of your own making with your cousin, as is your usual wont. How was I to know that on this particular day you had remained at home?"

Julie could not answer; instead she flounced over to the window to stand gazing over the cobbled mews to the stables.

"Will you not change your mind, to please me?" asked the duke cajolingly, coming to stand behind her.

"I tell you no, sir," she replied, sullenly attempting to move away, but he restrained her. "Let me go, Marcel," she pleaded. "I would return to my room."

"Not until you see what birthday gift I have for you, love," he said softly, speaking almost in her ear. Giving a sign to a groom awaiting his command in the stable yard, he watched his wife's face as a beautiful bay mare was led into the cobbled square.

Unable to speak, Julie watched the mare's progress until she stood before the window, her flaxen mane and tail moving gently in the summer breeze, her small, intelligent head rubbing against the groom's shoulder.

"I have named her Willow," said the duke softly, "but if you have a mind, you shall have the naming of her."

"It shall be Willow," breathed Julie, hardly able to tear her eyes from the horse. "It suits her so well."

"Have I chosen rightly?" he asked, as, eyes bright, she turned to face him.

"Thank you," she breathed, not trusting herself to say more, her softened features giving him his answer.

Realizing the danger of such a move, Marcel resisted the impulse to hold her to him and drew slightly away, saying, "Then away with you, madam wife, and change. We ride to Hyde Park together."

She was halfway across the room when she gave a guilty start. "I am promised to ride with John at four."

"My love, today your most estimable cousin can go to the devil. You will write him a note, if you must a polite one, explaining that you ride with your husband. I believe I hold precedence today."

"Yes, Marcel," she beamed and sped to her apartments.

To those who frequented the park, it was an unusual sight to see the Duke and Duchess of Lear riding side by side, he on a large chestnut stallion reputed to be named Satanas, and she on a delicately stepping bay mare. So used had they become to the duke's absence that the couple's progress around the park was marked by many stares, some of the young bucks even going so far as to quite openly stand agape.

Perfectly under control, Satanas, with well-muscled neck arched, side-stepped along the path. Keeping but a light hand on the reins, Marcel was fully aware of the sensation they were causing and felt a great surge of pride in the wife at his side. Julie, dressed in a habit of black velvet cut on military lines and a small chip hat, sat easily erect in the saddle. The mare responding to her every aid was a joy to ride.

It would seem at each turning they were required to halt to acknowledge some acquaintance, so their progress was necessarily slow, giving them no opportunity for conversation until, as they left the park and started to ride slowly homeward, the duke asked lightly, "I trust you have no engagements for this evening, my dear?"

Julie colored slightly at his tone. "I am engaged to dine with Lady Augusta and then accompany her party to Drury Lane. I had thought you to be going to your club, as is your usual wont."

"A ruse, love," smiled the duke. "Augusta will release you if you so wish. I had thought that on such an occasion you might dine with me and then, if you prefer, I am sure we could join Augusta's party later."

She smiled shyly in response. "I would like that above everything."

"By-the-bye, does Sir John go?" asked the duke casually.

"But of course," she gurgled, and, pushing the mare forward, urged her into a trot.

Carefully choosing a gown of midnight blue over a delicate underskirt embroidered with silver, Julie glowed with a happiness that had eluded her over the past two months. Delicate slippers of silver with jewel-studded heels adorned her feet to peep prettily from beneath her gown. Tonight she would wear her hair unpowdered, with only a silver ribbon threaded through the curls, though she would allow her maid to add a little color to her cheeks and salve to her lips. A necklace of sapphires and diamonds lay upon her breast, catching the light from the flickering candles.

Slowly she descended the stairs to join the duke in the drawing room, a pulse beating in the base of her throat and a slight fluttering of her hands betraying her apprehension. Cautiously opening the door, she found the duke, having forestalled her, was filling his glass from a crystal decanter. At sight of his wife, he laid both aside to greet her.

He, too, had taken care in his dressing, wearing an elegantly skirted coat and satin knee breeches of burgundy, with a waistcoat of dull gold brocade and gold lacing adorning his wide cuffs.

"I have instructed that the covers be laid in the small salon, love," he said, bowing low over her hand and carrying it to his lips. "It is fitting that on such an occasion we should forgo the grandeur of the dining room for a cozier atmosphere." Drawing her hand through his arm, he led the way toward the rear of the house.

Of necessity, the conversation remained on a general level while the lackeys brought in each course. Julie, for some reason, almost dreaded their departure, as she found it difficult to face the duke on this new, familiar footing. She was only too aware that her defenses were no proof against his attack, for here again was the man she had married.

When at last the covers were removed and the lackeys dismissed, the duke sat over his port, his eyes never leaving his wife's face and, reaching across the table, took her hand. "Am I so terrible, love?" he asked softly. "Would it be so difficult to forgive me?"

She drew her hand away; it would not do

to capitulate too readily. How could she tell him that she had forgiven him long ago, and that it was only the uncertainty of his affection that now stood between them?

"You are still something of a mystery to me, sir," she said lightly, averting her gaze, "and it is not my desire to merely be counted as a conquest."

"Never that," he said, frowning. "It would seem I have difficulty in shedding my past but, given the chance, Julie, I would wish to prove you wrong."

Unable to resist the emotion she saw in his eyes, she rose from the table, saying, "I think it is time we joined Lady Augusta, sir. As it is, we will miss the first act."

"As you will, my love," he conceded, perceiving the weakening of her defenses. Not wishing to jeopardize his position, and fully aware of the need for caution, he nonetheless felt greatly encouraged.

His affections for his wife had in no way lessened since their marriage, and it was with a feeling of triumph that he felt her hand slip into his as they drove toward Drury Lane.

With a welcoming smile, Lady Augusta gestured to them to be seated as they entered her box at the beginning of the second act. As the duke took his place beside her, she whispered, "I did not look to see you here, Marcel. Was it Julie's doing?"

"As you see, I accompany my wife," replied the duke with a meaningful smile. "I promise you, Augusta, not even Sir John's presence will put me out of frame tonight."

"Glad to hear it," she said and chuckled. "It would seem you may have won the day after all."

"Not quite, but I have hopes."

Lady Augusta made a sound of frustration. "If I know the chit, she probably forgave you this month past, and if you didn't go around with such a superior air, you'd have seen it yourself. Always did have too much self-consequence."

"I might have known you'd read me a lecture, Augusta," he said, smiling wryly. "But not even that will put me out of sorts this night."

"That's the trivet," approved her ladyship. "Now pay attention to this wretched comedy. It must seem we understand the cursed thing, though I vow even the players are lost."

Julie, having taken the seat proffered by her cousin, was seated at her ladyship's other side; Sir John, by needs of the box being crowded, was forced to stand behind her chair with two other gentlemen of the party. One look at his cousin's radiant countenance, however, and he had a fair grasp of the situation, causing him to be aware of no small amount of jealousy.

The farce continued, more hilarious from its mishaps than its dialogue. The audience in the pit became exceedingly noisy and in part drowned the actors' speech, but this in no way detracted from their enjoyment. Casting her gaze around the boxes to see what other notables were present, Julie became aware that she was the object of scrutiny from the box almost directly opposite. Here sat a fair beauty dressed in shades of blue, her gown cut exceedingly low to reveal her obvious charms, and Julie returned her stare with equal curiosity. She tried vainly to attract the duke's attention to ask the stranger's identity but, seeing the lady leave the box on the arm of her gallant, lost all interest and returned to the play.

At the end of the second act, Lady Augusta called for refreshments. Her party being so large, the lackeys had great difficulty in serving them, and reaching his wife's side, the duke suggested that they should step out into the corridor. "For, my dear," he confided, "I find the press unbearable."

Julie agreed and gratefully allowed him to lead her out of the box, leaving Lady Augusta to hold court among the young gallants present who found her wit excessively amusing.

The corridors seemed hardly less crowded than the box, the only consolation being that the throng was constantly moving. The duke drew Julie's hand through his arm, suggesting that they should seek refreshment in one of the anterooms, but even these seemed full to overflowing.

"It would seem the whole of London society bears us company this night," he drawled, raising his quizzing glass to survey the throng. "I think 'twould be best should we present our apologies to Augusta and return home."

"Could we not see just one more act, Marcel?" pleaded Julie. "I find it *fort amusement,* especially with all the interruptions from the pit."

"Pon faith, you have a very strange humor, love," said the duke, chuckling. "One more act and no more. Then we consign what is left to the devil. Forswear, I will suffer no more!"

"Thank you," she said and dimpled up at him. She would have said more, but the bell rang for the third act, and they were caught up in the press, each hurrying to their seats before the curtain should rise.

Foolishly, for a moment, Julie allowed her hand to slip from the duke's arm and in that instant was carried away in the crowd, seeing her husband disappearing in the opposite direction as they vainly attempted to reach each other. For a moment, she knew no small amount of panic, with a fear of suffocation from the converging throng.

Of a sudden, as if by design, the sea of bodies parted, and at the end of the corridor stood the duke with the fair beauty from the opposite box fixed firmly upon his arm, his head bent toward her attentively.

"It would seem Lear has not changed his ways, for all his recent nuptials," sneered a young gallant behind her, his rolling gait proclaiming his inebriation.

"Can't blame him," replied his companion. "I've heard tell The Dove was incomparable, and, now I see her in the flesh, I see they do not exaggerate. He must be in her toils for her to approach him so openly at a public event."

Feeling as if the world had dropped from beneath her feet, Julie stood unable to tear her eyes from the scene before her, and then, as the duke raised his head to meet her gaze, she gave a smothered cry. Without waiting to see his reaction, she ran along the now-empty corridor, down the wide steps to the foyer, and out into the cold night air.

The duke swore softly and long and, shaking the beauty's hand from his arm, attempted to follow his wife, but he was held back by sensuous arms, as clinging as any vine. Had Julie been privileged to hear their previous conversation — The Dove's pleas that the duke should settle her gaming debts and his flat refusal to do so — she would have perhaps realized in part the real state of affairs, but as she had not, how wide the gulf now?

Bodily flinging The Dove from him, the duke fixed her with a look of such loathing that she shrank back against the wall, hands pressed against it for support, and watched as he ran down the stairs in the wake of his wife. Despite his haste, he arrived at the entrance just in time to see his carriage being driven away at some speed.

Being admitted to Blake House some short while later, after making the journey in a hired conveyance, he made all possible haste to his wife's apartments, vowing to see Julie and make her understand. Flinging open her sitting room door, he found all to be in darkness, his fevered gaze confirming it to be empty. Realizing she must have retired to her bedchamber, he strode over to the adjoining door, the sound of uncontrollable sobbing halting him in his tracks. He paused for a moment, hand poised above the handle, but then, attempting to open the door, found it to be locked.

"Julie," he called softly through the shuttered door. "It is not what you think, sweetheart. I would explain if you would but hear me."

But there came no answer, only a slight muffling of the sobs, and, letting his hand drop from the lock, he turned away, slowly retracing his steps to the brightly lit landing. It would appear once more that the fates were against him.

CHAPTER SIXTEEN

For all his calm exterior, it needed only one look at the duke's ravaged countenance to see that he had spent a sleepless night, his eyes holding an almost haunted expression in their dark depths. Scorning breakfast, he immediately retreated to his study and, with the aid of his secretary, sorted through the morning's post, putting aside all but the most urgent business matters. His secretary, Hallsworth, aware of his employer's preoccupation, attempted to go about his tasks as unobtrusively as possible, laying matters carefully before the duke in order of precedence, invitations to routs and balls lying forgotten on his own desk.

His grace, giving only half a mind to the correspondence before him, raised his head expectantly at each light footstep heard to cross the hall, only to be the more dejected when its owner proved to be nothing more than a maid going about her tasks.

Hallsworth, aware that the duke found the morning's duties irksome, suggested completing the task for him and was rewarded by a curt word of thanks as the duke rose purposefully from his desk and strode to his wife's apartments.

She shall listen to me, he thought savagely. *It is within my power to make her do so.* Then contritely: *God, how I have hurt her. That she should be subjected to such treatment is unforgivable. I had thought yesterday we were beginning anew, but it would seem my past entraps me!*

Not waiting for a reply to his knock, the duke flung open the door to Julie's sitting room to find her reposing dejectedly by the window, still clad in a primrose wrapper that, at the sight of him, she drew tighter about her slender figure, as if for protection.

"You intrude, sir," she said, facing him coldly. "You enter my apartments by mistake."

"I assure you it is no mistake, *mignonne,*" he replied softly. "I come that you might listen to me."

"I see not the need," she replied tersely, rising to pace between window and hearth. "It would seem you have made the situation quite clear. The Dove looked so well upon your arm, as if she belonged there."

The duke turned away, unable to face the scorn in her eyes. "*Nom de Dieu,* am I never to escape this tangle? I swear to you, my love, by all that I hold sacred, I have never been involved with this woman. She casts out lures that I constantly ignore, but this time, it was a plea for funds to settle her gaming debts. She is desperate and sees me as a man of fortune, but I will have none of her."

"La, sir, you suppose I should be so easily hoodwinked? Last night, I overheard a conversation claiming her as your mistress."

"And you take their word over mine?"

"Is that what you would have me believe, after last night?"

"I give you my word, she is not!"

"Then, sir, you credit me for a bigger fool than I am!"

In that moment, the duke's temper snapped, and in one stride he bridged the distance between them, grasping her shoulders and forcing her to look at him. His fingers bit into her soft flesh, causing her to wince at their pressure, but he paid no heed.

"Madam, you drive me too far," he seethed, in no way relenting his hold. "I would cajole you, plead with you, entreat you, but you mock me. If you loved me as I love you, you would hear me out."

"Love me?" scorned Julie, meeting his fiery gaze. "Is it to love me to consort with females of the demimonde? To trick me into a marriage of convenience to suit the king? I tell you, sir, if I thought you indeed loved me, then would I ask you your motives?"

Snatching her to him, the duke kissed her savagely. "That is my motive," he said harshly, releasing her. "Do you now think it a marriage of convenience? In what way can I convince you?"

"J'vous hain," she breathed, visibly shaken, averting her face and pressing her hands against his chest as if to ward off any further embrace. "What of the girl in the Cyprian Hall?" she asked. "Am I to take no account of that, also?"

The duke dropped his hold on her. "It would seem you are remarkably well informed," he drawled. "I compliment you, madam. Your informant has been extremely thorough. It was a chance meeting, no more. A mild flirtation that had disastrous results. I see I waste my time. It would take more than I have within my power to convince you, but I would ask again, who is your informant and what motive do they have? Forswear, they have dealt me a damnable blow."

"I know not the woman's identity," she replied, holding on to the back of the couch for support. "She said she was but a messenger for a mutual acquaintance who bore you no love."

"That, *mon ami,* could be half of society," scoffed the duke. "It would seem my forte is to inspire enmity! But, be warned, madam wife, I do not relinquish you so readily. Though you may think you hate me now, I have reason to think you not as indifferent as you would have me believe. I once had your love, of that I am certain, and there will be a time when I will have it again!" With this, he stormed from the room and down to the hallway, calling for Satanas as he went.

Trembling, and with tears stealing from beneath closed lids, Julie sank to the couch, her flaming cheeks cradled in her ice-cold hands. He had said he loved her, but it was not the declaration she would have looked for, and instinctively she knew that he had been driven beyond endurance. She doubted not her own devotion, but with each new set of events, confusion reigned, and she felt her heart would break.

If previously the duke had been noted by his absence, it would now seem he paid marked attendance to any entertainment of his wife's devising, thoroughly disconcerting the young gallants who would pay her court. None was more surprised than Julie herself at the turn of events, for, while he in no way put himself forward, his very presence seemed to fill a room, his eyes to follow her every movement.

Standing slightly aloof from the other guests, his very height making him noticeable, he eyed the throng through his quizzing glass as they arrived at Blake House for a soirée. As to be expected, Sir John was one of the first to arrive, his smile fading slightly at sight of his host.

"An unusual occasion," he said, approaching the duke with hand extended. "I would not have supposed a soirée to your liking."

"Then, my friend, it shows how little you know me," drawled the duke, taking John's proffered hand in the briefest of salutes. "It would seem I have neglected my wife far too long when it becomes a matter for comment that I should be present in my own home."

"I am pleased you are aware of it," retorted Sir John. "It is not pleasant to see my cousin so slighted as to be left without a host."

"A position you have been happy to fill until this night," replied his grace, barely concealing his mood. "But have no fear, I will not intrude upon her dependence on your company. If she turns to me, it will be of her own accord. I wish not to play on her sentiments."

"Sir, if you are suggesting —"

"I suggest nothing," said the duke, smiling. "I but merely state fact."

From across the room, Julie saw the duke move away from her cousin to greet a recently arrived acquaintance and engage him in conversation, his bearing everything that was amiable in a host. Finding Sir John at her side, she laid her hand on his arm.

"What brings Marcel here tonight?" she asked. "I had thought him at his club."

"I know not what brings him," snapped Sir John, "but he seems set on being cursed unpleasant."

Julie chuckled. "Has he put your nose out of joint already, John? I'm not surprised, if you looked at him with such a sour countenance. It almost puts me to fright."

Moving slightly away, he proffered a curt bow. "I had not thought I displeased to that extent," he said shortly, offense showing clearly in every line. "It would seem, ma'am, that you and your husband are singularly well suited this night."

Julie's eyes narrowed slightly. "You would

do well to remember that he is my husband, John," she said coldly, "and this is his house, to which, until this moment, you have been a welcome visitor. I would not wish in future to have to deny you entry because of a silly squabble."

"That, dear cousin, is entirely in your hands," he replied stiffly, "and I can see that now that you have your husband's company, mine is no longer needed."

Perceiving the humor of the situation, Julie gave a chuckle. "It would seem we are quarrelling like children again, and I am far too mystified by Marcel's motives to wish to argue with you. Is it not most intriguing?"

"You may find it so, but I do not," replied Sir John, still not in the best of humors. "He seems to delight in putting me out of countenance."

"Only because you let him do so."

"And what else, ma'am, am I supposed to do? Serve him a leveler?"

"I doubt that you could," she replied with some aplomb, moving away from him to welcome Lady Quinn.

Finding himself bearing Lady Augusta's company, the duke raised her hand to his lips. "As you see, dear aunt, I do as you bid," he said and smiled.

"I had thought you already to have come about," she replied, frowning, "and then you allow yourself to be seen with a light-skirt on your arm. I'm thoroughly out of patience with you, Marcel, make no mistake. I had credited you with more sense!"

The duke mirrored her frown. "News travels fast. I had not thought my actions so worthy of comment. It was a plea for funds, no more." Then, brightening: "But at least now I see some hope. I was all at sea. Then it struck me — it can't really be over between us, or why else should Julie be jealous? In fact, Augusta, it has breathed new life into me, and, to use your own phrase, I woo the chit. At the moment, it needs be from a distance. She must come to me willingly. Of a sudden, I knew all was not at an end, so now you see me dancing attendance on my own wife. Novel, is it not?"

"Anything that would have you tamed is novel," she said, chuckling dryly. "I wish you well. I hope she leads you a regular bear dance. It would only be your true desserts."

He grinned. "Of that you can be quite sure. Nonetheless, it would seem I have Austin in retreat already."

"And about time too. You'd not be worth your salt if you failed in that task."

"It is not my intention to fail in any task, Aunt."

"Humph! Then it's time you looked to your laurels, my boy."

"As ever, Augusta, you are right!"

Seeing his wife unattended some short while later, the duke took the opportunity to draw her aside. "You do well tonight, love," he said. "Everything as it should be. You make a charming hostess. I congratulate you. However, it would seem I have needs to offer my apologies should my presence have robbed you of the court of the many beaux you are reputed to have in your toils."

She was about to give a hasty retort but, seeing the amused twinkle in his eye, refused to rise to the bait and instead replied sweetly, "It is good to have one's efforts appreciated. I thank you. As for beaux, sir, you exaggerate."

"I assure you, my dear, I do not," he said and smiled. "I am the envy of society. Could it be that you are oblivious of the admiration you inspire?"

"I do not wish for admiration."

"Do you not?" he asked quizzically.

"No!"

"Then I see there are many here tonight doomed for disappointment."

"And am I to include you among their

242

ranks, Marcel?" she asked sarcastically.

"But of course, my love," he replied silkily, sweeping her a deep bow.

To Lady Augusta, viewing them from afar, their actions seemed strange. *If that is courtship, then I am getting very old,* she thought, chuckling to herself. *Can't say but what I envy them though, if I were only fifty years younger . . . but then, I'm not, and pon rep, I would not have changed my youth!*

As the evening neared its end and the first of the guests began their leave-taking, Lady Roxborough, one of the queen's ladies in waiting, sought Julie out to add her congratulations to those of the duke.

She smiled, taking Julie's hand in hers. "A most enjoyable evening, my dear. I foresee you to have a great future as a hostess. It must be arranged for you to be presented at court. Her Majesty will be delighted. It is already seen that your parties become the rage, and the queen has taken quite an interest in you."

"A fact that is hardly surprising," replied Julie coolly, withdrawing her hand from Lady Roxborough's clasp.

Her ladyship, extremely puzzled by this reaction, said, "Her Majesty was greatly pleased by your marriage. Should it be thought strange that she should now follow your progress with some interest?"

"Your ladyship, I am quite aware of the queen's dealings in my marriage," said Julie stiffly, "but I find it unkind that you should needs remind me of it at such a time."

"I know not your meaning," replied her ladyship, thoroughly at sea, "and if I have by some chance word inadvertently offended you, I apologize."

"Have no fear," said Julie, drawing herself aloof to hide the imaginary hurt. "I have been thoroughly apprised that my marriage was ordered by the Crown," and, sweeping a deep curtsy, she made her departure, leaving a completely bemused Lady Roxborough to stare after her in some confusion. Her ladyship made a mental note to arrange a *tête-à-tête* with her old friend Augusta as soon as engagements would allow to see if she could throw any light on the situation, for obviously matters were not as they should be.

CHAPTER SEVENTEEN

Those of the duke's acquaintance who looked for him at his clubs or the more select of the gaming establishments were doomed for disappointment. In fact, to some of his cronies it would seem that he had disappeared from the face of the earth. Instead, to the curiosity of many and great surprise of all, he was to be seen squiring his wife on every fashionable occasion, leaving her side only on matters of business. No attention seemed too trivial, no amusement too boring. Rondos, soirées, card parties, musical evenings — all received his undivided attention, his marked preference for his wife's company bordering on the unfashionable.

The news that Lord Carlisle was on the market to sell his matching pair of blood-chestnuts, however, proved just too tempting an event to overlook. Informing his wife of his intentions to drive down to the

Carlisle estates, he rose early and set out immediately after taking breakfast. For once, Julie had no social engagements; therefore, she was free to spend the day as she chose, and midmorning she decided to call into a select little milliner's that was reputed to have an array of fashionable new imports from Paris.

As the day progressed, she became aware of an impatience for her husband's return but, knowing not to expect him until quite late, she resigned herself to what would seem a lengthy evening. Of late, there had started to exist a certain ease in each other's company that had been absent for quite some time. It would seem that the duke's attentions had indeed started to show some rewards, although Julie still found it difficult to drop her guard, and their meetings still remained on a politely formal footing.

The shadows lengthened, and she dined alone before repairing to the drawing room with some books. She rejected each one in turn, finding in none the diversion she sought. Suddenly, as the mantel clock chimed the hour of ten, the sound of impatient horses being halted before the front door sent her flying to investigate, throwing wide the heavy curtain the better to observe the new arrival.

It was a moment before she could compre-hend the scene before her. A post chaise, liberally spattered with mud, was halted before the stone steps — not her husband's curricle, as she had hoped to see. As the post-boy jumped down from his box to open the door, it was flung open by the oc-cupant, and a much travel-weary Stefan alighted, shaking out his crumpled ruffles and straightening his cravat before mount-ing the steps. Being guilty of a momentary disappointment, Julie ran to greet the traveler as a lackey gave him access.

"My dear duchess," said Stefan, entering the hallway and making a magnificent leg. "As radiant as ever, I see."

"Fie on you," she blushed, advancing to meet him, hand outstretched to receive his salute. " 'Tis monstrous good to see you. We had not expected you until Christmas. Marcel will be delighted. He drove down to Lord Carlisle's estates this morning intent on purchasing a new pair of carriage horses, but I have expected his return anytime this past hour or more. I know not what delays him."

"I hope you will excuse my coming to you straight from the road m'dear," said Stefan, indicating his travel-stained state, "but I was hoping you would afford me lodgings until the morrow, when I will travel to my estates. Also, if possible, I needs have speech with Marcel before I retreat to the country."

"You are welcome to stay as long as you like," said Julie with a smile, leading the way into the drawing room, where Stefan eased himself thankfully into a large, comfortable chair.

"Curse that post chaise," he said, stretching his aching limbs. "Forswear it was so ill sprung it would be better termed a bone breaker. And the Channel — I shudder at the memory." He dabbed at his brow with a lace handkerchief as if the mere thought of it proved too much for his delicate senses.

Ringing for the lackey, Julie requested refreshment for the recently arrived traveler, herself providing him with a glass of claret from a decanter set on a side table.

Taking the glass from her hand, Stefan remarked, "You are looking exceedingly well, dear cousin. Could it be that London agrees with you?"

"I am beginning to think that it may," replied Julie demurely, "but tell me, Stefan, what brings you back so soon?"

"A matter of business," he replied carelessly, as if indifferent to the subject. "I find Paris strangely boring. Everyone, it would seem, has returned to England. I but follow the trend. The capital is almost devoid of entertainment and is exceedingly dull."

"Then you must stay with us for the remainder of the season," she said and smiled. "We at least can offer you some diversion."

"I doubt Marcel would welcome my intrusion," said Stefan with a chuckle. "Not at all the thing. Hardly been married a six-month. No, better open up my own establishment. I will not trespass on your newly married state. He would not wish me to."

Julie's blushes were saved by the entrance of a lackey bearing a large silver tray with the required refreshments, which he set on the small table at the visitor's elbow. Stefan fell to immediately. "You will forgive me, my dear," he said and grinned, attacking a portion of capon, "but the rigors of the journey leave me ravenous. It is an age since we stopped for nuncheon."

"I am only pleased that you find our humble offerings to your liking," said Julie with a chuckle, amused by her companion's enthusiasm for the meal. "Now, if you will excuse me for a moment, I will see to the ordering of your bedchamber."

It was almost midnight. Stefan, having changed his travel-stained raiment for a suit of amber satin, sat playing a hand or two of piquet with Julie, who was unable to give the game her full attention, as she constantly rose at the slightest sound to peer into the empty street. Suddenly, the unmistakable clatter of hooves sounded outside, and the duke's voice could be heard ordering his groom to stable the horses.

Gathering her skirts, Julie ran out into the hall and would have flung the door wide herself had not the lackey forestalled her, bowing low as the duke entered. She had not realized just how anxious she had become because of his lateness but checked the impulse to run to him — it would not do. Instead, she stood in the shadows of the staircase. Her presence did not go unnoticed, however, and, striding forward, the duke took both her hands in his.

"You need not have waited up for me, love," he said, slightly perplexed, noticing the color mount her cheeks. "I was delayed on the road. One of the wheelers threw lame, and I needs go slowly until he was replaced."

"I wanted to see you safely returned. That is all," she said hesitantly, refusing to meet his questioning gaze as she disengaged her hands from his clasp. "But where are my wits? Marcel, you have a visitor. Stefan has returned from Paris and is eager to see you."

"Whatever brings him back to London so early? I was not looking to see him until the end of the year," pondered the duke aloud. He was still confused by his wife's greeting, the look in her eyes arresting him, but if Stefan was waiting, he could pursue it no further and instead reached out and drew her hand through his arm, clamping it to his side before she could withdraw it. "Come, my dear, we will show him what a devoted couple we have become," he said, smiling, and led the way into the drawing room to meet his cousin.

After only a short while in their company, Julie decided that it would be prudent to leave the two cousins to their discussions, as the hour was late and her vigilance had made her weary. Therefore, making her excuses and ignoring their protestations, she retired to her own apartments, not realizing until she reached her bedchamber that she had been left with a feeling of disappointment at having to relinquish her husband's company so soon. She would have to school her emotions. It would not do that she should seem eager to seek his attention. Realizing that in her actions she had almost given herself away, she vowed to be on her guard.

■ ■ ■ ■

In the drawing room below, the cousins sat at their ease over an excellent bottle of port, the lateness of the hour affecting them not.

"Marriage sits you well, Marcel," said Stefan, eyeing the duke over the rim of his glass. "I congratulate you." Then after a slight hesitation: "Fact is, Marcel, if truth be told, it is an institution I contemplate myself."

"Nom de Dieu," expostulated the duke, laughing and sitting upright in his chair. "I had thought you to be a confirmed bachelor. Who nose-leads you to the altar? Forswear, there was no sign of a bride when I was in Paris."

"Saphina Charsley."

"It is not a name I know," replied the duke thoughtfully.

"I would not expect you to. In the eyes of the world she is a nobody, but to me — never!" said Stefan with some force. "She travels as companion to the Duchess of Wimborne and suffers damnably at her hands."

"And you see yourself as her knight in shining *amour*," said the duke, chuckling. "Certainly a new role for you, and not one

I would have suspected you of taking on willingly!"

"Nothing of the sort," replied Stefan indignantly, as he rose to refill his glass. "She is the sweetest of all creatures. One could not help but feel protective toward her, but having once pledged her company, she will not leave the duchess until she has completed the Grand Tour. So I return to my estates to prepare them for her coming. Saphina has asked me to keep our betrothal a secret until she herself is able to return to England, for fear I should think better of contracting such an alliance, but I tell you, Marcel, I am in deadly earnest. I will have her to wife. I care not for opinion."

"I congratulate you, cousin," said the duke with a smile, raising his glass in salute. "She would seem an estimable bride. I wish you well."

Stefan colored with pride. "I thank you. My reason for coming is to ask if she can come to you on her return from the continent. She has no family, and it would be flaunting propriety should she come to me at my bachelor abode before we are wed. I wish everything to be as it should, not a breath of scandal. I have not spoken to Julie on the matter until I have your permission to do so."

"Your Saphina is more than welcome," said the duke. "When can we look for her return?"

"Sometime in December."

"And your wedding?"

"Upon her return, by special license."

"I see then, coz, you intend no time to be lost," said the duke with a chuckle. "It would seem you are eager to set up your nursery."

"As eager as any man," replied Stefan. "And by-the-bye, I would have supposed you to be in a fair way of establishing your own by now."

"Just so," replied the duke, all humor fading and showing no desire whatsoever to expand upon the subject.

Oblivious of the change in the duke's mood, Stefan continued much in the same vein, extolling the virtues of his bride, recalling their meeting and subsequent courtship until a sudden thought struck him, making him sit forward in his chair.

"Eh, God, knew there was something I wanted to tell you, coz," he said eagerly.

"And what pray is that?" inquired the duke, becoming bored with his companion's narrative and making as if to rise.

"Now don't fix me with that jaundiced eye. This is something you will definitely appreciate, Marcel. Your old adversary Coustellet is dead!"

"What!" expostulated the duke uncomprehendingly, sitting back in his chair, and then mockingly: "Don't tell me he has been involved in yet another scandal resulting in a duel?"

"Debtor's prison," replied Stefan gleefully. "Couldn't pay his debts. Flung into prison two months since."

"Never known anyone to be executed for their debts."

"Not executed," returned Stefan, impatiently. "Fell foul of an inmate. Murdered!"

"A very fitting end," purred the duke, with some satisfaction, as he emptied his wineglass. "What better settling of scores could I have wished for?"

"One thing remains a mystery to me, Marcel. Could never explain it."

"And that is?"

"Day of your wedding, met Caroline at the reception. Heard tell from a guest later that she was under Coustellet's protection. How gained she entry to the event?"

"I know not," replied the duke absentmindedly, still contemplating his adversary's demise and not recognizing a connection. "After she left your protection, all those years ago, I have taken no interest in her whatsoever. I rescued you from her clutches, and, as far as I was concerned, the matter was closed. They made a very well-suited pair."

"You may well say that," countered Stefan. "It was she who ran through his fortune, or so it is said. Left him too, by God, as soon as the funds ran out, so it would seem he has been very well repaid."

"A score well settled," agreed the duke, with great appreciation of the situation. "The malicious, money-grabbing mistress I helped you discard ruins my enemy without being aware of the service she has performed on my behalf. Very droll."

"Thought you would see the irony of it," said Stefan with a grin. "Now, if you will excuse me, I will seek my bed. I stay only until morning and then return to Ramblings. I must assure that everything is in readiness for my bride."

"Then I wish you *bonne nuit*. I remain a moment longer," replied the duke, appearing deep in thought. "We can make whatever arrangements are necessary before your departure on the morrow. Julie will be delighted with your news, I am sure."

Stefan left his cousin to his deliberations and retired to his bedchamber with thoughts of his bride uppermost in his mind. The duke, however, was not so eager to seek his repose. Instead, he refilled his glass, to sit musing over the evening's revelations, not least of all being the fact that Julie had appeared to have been eager for his return.

After a short while, he rose abruptly, as if reaching a decision, and purposefully made his way into the hall and up the staircase to pause outside his wife's apartments with hand raised toward the latch. Dare he jeopardize the ease that had started to exist between them by entering? He was unsure. The hall clock chiming the hour of three made him start, however, and he let drop his arm once more to his side, reasoning that if she had intended to further their conversation she would not have excused herself so readily from his company. Nor have been so keen to retire.

Convincing himself that whatever eagerness for his return he had thought he had perceived had been only a figment of his own willing imagination, he made his way to his bedchamber, chiding himself for being a fool. He would not endanger their reconciliation. Too much was at stake, and it was too soon to take such a risk. Whatever ground he had gained in their relationship could so easily be lost. He must be more certain before hazarding more.

CHAPTER EIGHTEEN

The results of Lady Roxborough having invited Lady Augusta to an afternoon coze were soon to be seen. His grace, having driven to Stovely the day after Stefan's departure to attend to matters of the estate, had been forced to leave his wife to her own devices for a few days. Julie sat reading in the drawing room when Lady Roxborough was announced and, hastily putting aside her book, found herself coloring with confusion, for she had almost immediately regretted her rudeness at their last meeting. Lady Roxborough, however, seemed not to notice as she advanced into the room, dressed in an elegant gown of cream silk decorated with knots of green. Lady Roxborough ignored Julie's outstretched hand and instead, taking her completely by surprise, kissed her cheek before drawing her to sit beside her ladyship on the couch.

"My dear, you must wonder at my visit,"

she began, seeing Julie's confusion.

"Oh, no, your ladyship," interrupted Julie, "but at our last meeting I was unforgivably rude, and I must beg your pardon . . ."

"Nonsense, my dear. I quite understand," Lady Roxborough replied, patting Julie's hand reassuringly. "Now, I will not prevaricate, my dear. I have come to set matters right. You have been grossly misled. Whoever told you that you had been entrapped into a marriage of convenience lied. Have no fear, I have the whole from Augusta — strictly in confidence, I do assure you. She was not able to put the situation to rights herself, but if you will listen to me, I hope that I may do so."

"There is no need," said Julie in muffled tones, attempting to hide her confusion.

"That, my love, is where you are quite wrong," replied her ladyship, taking firm control of the situation. "I was with the queen when she received a reply from your husband stating his intention to take you to wife. Admittedly, Their Majesties were of the opinion that he should marry, even going so far as to have chosen a bride for him, but his grace would have none of it. His letter was correct and declared that he was conscious of his duty and allegiance to the Crown, in fact everything such a letter should be, but he avowed to take you to wife, even if Their Majesties disapproved and it necessitated his exile. Stating, in fact, that he would rather remain in France with you than return home to England without you. Of course, Their Majesties were delighted. They wholeheartedly approved of his choice. Who would not, especially as he stated his cause so passionately?

"Already it has become apparent that you have been the saving of him, has it not? Forswear, he has become a changed man, my dear. Now, what's to do? Why are you crying? Is what I have said so terrible? For I promise you, it is the truth."

"Madame, I have acted so stupidly," said Julie through her tears. "I have listened to others and taken their word when I should have heeded my husband. I wouldn't even believe him when he pleaded with me, so unsure had I let myself become of his affections, and I have allowed a situation to exist that should have been resolved months ago. I have behaved as a fool. I just pray that it is not too late to make amends."

"Nonsense," chided her ladyship, patting Julie's hand. "I have it from Augusta that the man is besotted with you. It has done him no harm to be brought to heel. But to whom have you been listening? Who was it

that put you on the wrong tack, and whatever their motives?"

"I neither know nor care, and haven't this
age," said Julie, dabbing at her eyes with a
lace handkerchief, and she told her companion of all that had transpired on her wedding day. "If only Marcel had attempted to
set matters right, or even said that he loved
me, none of this would have come to pass,
but he withdrew into that remoteness he so
often affects, so what was I to suppose?"

"La, my love, that husband of yours was
always a scoundrel," said her ladyship, "but
what man worth his salt is not? The man is
nine-and-twenty. Would you expect of him
an unblemished past? Is it not enough that
he came to you with a pure heart, for none
had touched that organ until you took his
defenses by storm." Then, looking over her
shoulder toward the door: "Where is he, by-
the-bye? I should not wish to come across
him and the motives for my visit become
known. It would not do for me to be found
out."

"He has gone to Stovely to see his agent,"
said Julie, with some dejection. "I am not
expecting his return for almost a week. I
wish now that it was sooner. It will seem an
age." Then, of a sudden, she brightened. "I
will go to Stovely," she said, rising on

impulse to pace the hearth. "He will not be looking to see me, and perhaps I can put matters right."

"But would you go unaccompanied?" asked her ladyship, somewhat surprised. "It is a fair way, and I am sure your husband would not be pleased that you should go alone. Would it not be better to await his return?"

"So has been the state of affairs that has existed between us over the last few months that to delay would be intolerable," said Julie, in some agitation. "I must speak to him before it is too late to repair the situation."

"Then I will take my leave," said her ladyship, rising and shaking out the folds in her skirt. "I have accomplished what I set out to achieve and must let you be about your arranging. Never let it be said that I was the cause of your delay." And on this Lady Roxborough made her departure, well content with the outcome of her visit, in fact an afternoon that had brought about the desired result.

Julie, however, was now thrown into a turmoil of emotions, alternating between elation and apprehension, but remaining firm in her resolve to journey to Stovely. If previously her husband had stated that he was determined to make her listen to his reasoning, she was now as fixed in her intentions to state her case, and she bade all to be in readiness for her departure at first light on the morrow.

CHAPTER NINETEEN

Leaving the confines of London shortly after dawn, the chaise sped swiftly forward onto the open road. Julie sat, a pale solitary figure in the corner of the coach, the effect of a sleepless night now showing clearly on her ashen countenance as she pressed herself into the shadows. She had refused breakfast. The thought of food had been obnoxious in her agitated state, and the length of the journey ahead of her did nothing to ease her anxiety; she was experiencing the full spectrum of emotions.

The coachman had assured her they should arrive at Stovely sometime in the late evening, and all her attention was directed toward this. The desire to see her husband being uppermost in her mind, she would not allow herself to dwell on the possibility of delay. She could not believe she had been so naïve as to have let the state of affairs come to such a pass. There had been opportunities over the past six months to have built bridges, but always some aspect of the situation had stood in the way. She alternatively pleated and smoothed the dark green skirts of her traveling habit in her agitation, and in her preoccupation with her thoughts did not notice as both the hours and surroundings sped by.

She had remained in the coach at each change of horses, preferring that the postillions should deal with such matters, and thus had had no thoughts of nuncheon. As the day wore on, the sleepless night and the length of the journey began taking their toll and she found that her lids were becoming exceedingly heavy, and allowing herself to relax against the squabs she drifted into an uneasy slumber.

It was some short time later, when the light had started to fail, that she was propelled into wakefulness and a deal of confusion by finding herself thrown into a heap on the floor of the chaise. The vehicle was now tipping at an alarming angle, the window of the opposite door being uppermost. Almost immediately, the face of a postillion appeared at the opening and, forcing the door open, he demanded to know if her grace was injured.

"As far as I can tell, I am but shaken," she

said, attempting to right herself so that she could accept his assistance to climb out of the open door. "What has happened? What is the cause of this calamity?" she demanded. "How fares the coachman and horses?" With the servant's aid, she managed to scramble through the opening and onto the roadside. The sight that met her eyes answered her question; the coach had plunged into a ditch, with both its offside wheels broken. The coachman seemed unhurt and was attempting to calm the wheeler, which appeared extremely lame.

"How far are we from Stovely?" she asked, pacing the lane, fretful now of the delay.

"It is about another two hours away, your grace," replied the postillion attempting to soothe the other horses, which would insist on plunging about in the confines of the narrow lane, and it taking all his efforts to try to bring about some calm. "Perhaps your grace would prefer to return to the posting inn we passed a short way down the road while we see what can be done to repair the coach, though I'm afraid we may not be able to put it to rights tonight."

Julie thought for a moment. She could not believe that her plans had been so easily thwarted, and tears of frustration stung her eyes. What now of her desire to reach her husband?

Perceiving the hopelessness of the situation, she said, "As it is so late, instead of attempting to repair the coach, perhaps it would be better if you should take a sound horse and ride to Stovely. There you must apprise my husband of the situation and ask him to send a coach for me on the morrow. I am sure he will know what is best to be done. I will retire to the inn and await your return. Nothing further can be done here for the moment. Just ensure that the horses are taken care of."

This was not how she would have chosen to arrive at Stovely, and her patience was not now at its best, but what could she do about the situation? It would seem that even now the fates were against her, and she was to be refused the outcome she desired!

Some short while later, Julie was safely ensconced in a private parlor at the White Hound, a large posting inn on the Portsmouth Road. The mantel clock had chimed the hour of eight. She suddenly became aware that it was more than twenty-four hours since she had last eaten and she ordered a light repast and a glass of wine to revive her. She stood before the fire, extending her hands to the warmth of the blaze in the hearth. It was almost October, and the evenings were becoming chill. It was therefore with no surprise that she heard the door open and the landlord bring in her supper.

Had she but known it, His Grace the Duke of Lear was at that moment receiving his groom in his office at Stovely.

"What's to do now?" he demanded in some surprise, putting aside the papers he was signing. "What brings you to Stovely? Is there a problem at Blake House?"

"I'm afraid there has been an accident with the chaise on the Portsmouth Road, sir," said the groom with some trepidation, "and her grace has sent me to inform you of the situation."

"What the deuce has my wife got to do with it?" snapped the duke, pushing his chair from the desk and hastily rising. "What was the chaise doing on the Portsmouth Road? Is she injured in any way? Come tell me, man."

"Her grace is unhurt, sir. The chaise went into a ditch, and I am afraid we were unable to repair it immediately, as both offside wheels are broken. Your wife is now waiting at the White Hound and asks if you would send the carriage for her in the morning."

"But why was it necessary for her to travel

down to Stovely?" asked the duke in some confusion. "I had thought her safely in London. What is wrong?"

"I know not, sir. All I know is that we were ordered to set out at first light this morning."

"Then I must go to her directly. Order my horse to be brought immediately, and then you can bring the carriage to us on the morrow. I must and will know the meaning of this and be assured that my wife is safe." With an irrational fear that something dire had come to pass, he left his office in some haste and no little perplexity to prepare for his journey, wondering why his wife should be following so hastily in his wake.

The events of the day had so exhausted Julie that she had fallen into a deep sleep on the settle before the roaring fire. So deep was her slumber that she was totally unaware of her husband's arrival. His grace, booted, spurred, and liberally covered in dust, thrust open the parlor door, a great anxiety showing on his ravaged countenance. In just three strides, he crossed the parlor floor, brooking the distance between them.

Falling to his knees beside the settle, he called her name softly, attempting to wake her, but so complete was her exhaustion that she only stirred a little, mumbling incoherently in her sleep, and then once more sank into its enveloping depths. Slightly reassured, he gave a heavy sigh and allowed some of the tension to seep from his being. Rising to his feet, he lifted her into his arms with a great gentleness, her head falling onto his shoulder, and, carrying her into the hallway, asked directions to her bedchamber. The landlord would have assisted him, but the duke was reluctant to release his precious burden and instead carried his wife to her apartment and gently laid her on the bed.

Closing the door, he took the chair from the hearth and placed it beside the bed, not wishing to lose sight of his sleeping charge. Pulling the coverlet over her slender figure and tenderly stroking the curls from her brow, he drew the chair even closer and took her hand in his.

"What are you at now, my love?" he chided softly, not wishing to wake her. "Why was it so necessary for you to travel to Stovely? I cannot bear the thought that you might have been injured in your haste. Now sleep, and I will bear you company. You can tell me all in the morning, and then we can see what is to be done. Have no fear;

whatever the problem, it can be resolved." So saying, he leaned back in the chair, his eyes never leaving his wife's face, marveling at her softened features as she slept, oblivious of his adoring scrutiny.

The gentle light of dawn slowly invaded the room, its tendrils touching Julie's cheek as she gradually became conscious of her surroundings and, turning her head on the pillow, became aware of the duke, now asleep, in the chair beside the bed, his hand resting on the quilt.

"Marcel, you came," she breathed, and immediately he was awake and kneeling at her side.

"How could I not, *mignonne?*" he asked softly, carrying her hand to his lips. His desire was to hold her, but he forced himself to be mindful not to overstep the imposed boundaries, boundaries that he wished to the devil. Then, with an attempt at the ordinary: "What the deuce possessed you to travel down to Stovely? If you had but said, I would have gladly taken you with me, but I thought you wished to remain in London. It was foolhardy to attempt the journey on your own and in such haste. The groom told me that you had set out at dawn. What matter was so urgent that it would not await my return?"

Faced now with uncertainty, Julie found it difficult to find the words. "My love, if you but knew," she said, smiling tentatively, not daring to look at his face for fear of what she might see. Had she done right?

Taken aback by her tone and endearment, his grace was completely nonplussed. This was a new state of affairs. Could he trust this small ray of hope that would rise and push its way into his consciousness? Instead, he returned to the chair.

"I will know, if you would but tell me," he said, attempting to hide behind a nonchalance he was far from feeling.

Throwing aside the coverlet and paying no heed to her crumpled state, Julie rose to stand before him, her hands fluttering nervously.

"Is it too late, Marcel?" she asked, her voice trembling with emotion. "Is it too late for me to make amends? Can you ever forgive my foolishness, my lack of understanding?" She held out her hand pleadingly toward him.

He took that hand eagerly and roughly pulled her onto his lap, but still he held her slightly away from him. "Are you saying what I have mind that you are saying, madam wife?" he asked, eyes alight but still unable to trust what thoughts tumbled into his head.

Somewhat heartened by his response, Julie rested her free hand against his cheek. "I am saying, my love, that which I should have said these months past. I care not what has gone before in your life — only that now we are together," and she watched the light of realization dawn on his face and rejoiced in it.

The duke gathered her to him. He knew not what had brought about this wondrous change — there would be time enough for that later. Instead, he said in her ear, "*Mignonne,* I have been waiting to take you to wife this many a while. Does this mean I now have a wife? Are you mine? Do you truly love me?"

For answer, she buried her face against his throat and, winding her arms about his neck, nodded and whispered, *"Tout mon etre."*

The duke gave a crow of delight, *"My wife!"* and the boundaries that had existed since the day of their marriage faded into oblivion.

The employees of Thorndike Press hope you have enjoyed this Large Print book. All our Thorndike, Wheeler, and Kennebec Large Print titles are designed for easy reading, and all our books are made to last. Other Thorndike Press Large Print books are available at your library, through selected bookstores, or directly from us.

For information about titles, please call:
    (800) 223-1244

or visit our Web site at:
    http://gale.cengage.com/thorndike

To share your comments, please write:
    Publisher
    Thorndike Press
    10 Water St., Suite 310
    Waterville, ME 04901